"You're here."

"I know." Matthew shrugged. "I couldn't stay away. I meant to, you know. I didn't want to be involved."

"Sometimes we don't have a choice," Parker replied, watching as he picked up a chair and brought it close.

Matthew settled down close to her, their shoulders touching. He leaned to watch as Faith slept in her arms. For a long time, the two of them sat in silence, both focused on the infant.

"She's much prettier today than she was yesterday," he said after a while. "I've always felt guilty, lying to parents and telling them their newborns are the cutest thing ever."

She laughed a little at the remark and Faith's eyes opened, seeking them with the tiniest turn of her head. Again, Parker wondered about her parents. Were they young? Was the mother okay?

"What will they do with her?" Matthew asked as he put his finger in her tiny hand and watched those fingers curl around his.

His question hurt, not that he intended that. She didn't want to think about Faith leaving, going to strangers. She didn't want to think about the short amount of time they—no, *she*—would have with this baby girl.

Brenda Minton lives in the Ozarks with her husband, children, cats, dogs and strays. She is a pastor's wife, Sunday-school teacher, coffee addict and is sleep-deprived. Not in that order. Her dream to be an author for Harlequin started somewhere in the pages of a romance novel about a young American woman stranded in a Spanish castle. Her dreams came true, and twenty-plus books later, she is an author hoping to inspire young girls to dream.

Books by Brenda Minton

Love Inspired

Her Small Town Secret
Her Christmas Dilemma
Earning Her Trust

Sunset Ridge

Reunited by the Baby

Mercy Ranch

Reunited with the Rancher
The Rancher's Christmas Match
Her Oklahoma Rancher
The Rancher's Holiday Hope
The Prodigal Cowboy
The Rancher's Holiday Arrangement

Visit the Author Profile page at LoveInspired.com for more titles.

Reunited by the Baby

Brenda Minton

ISBN-13: 978-1-335-58562-2

Reunited by the Baby

For questions and comments about the quality of this book, please contact us at CustomerService@Harlequin.com.

Love Inspired
22 Adelaide St. West, 41st Floor
Toronto, Ontario M5H 4E3, Canada
www.LoveInspired.com

Printed in U.S.A.

He that dwelleth in the secret place of the most High shall abide under the shadow of the Almighty. I will say of the Lord, He is my refuge and my fortress: my God; in him will I trust.

—*Psalm* 91:1-2

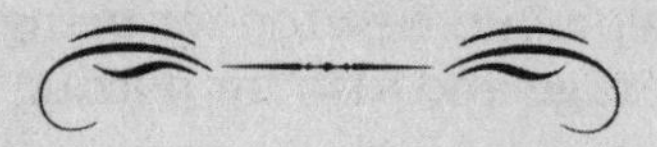

The truth about writing. Some books are a little more difficult to write. Some books, like children, take a village. I want to thank the editors at Love Inspired for patience and guidance in this process. Thank you to my agent, Melissa Jeglinski, for a calm voice in the storm. And to Stephanie Newton for being willing to read, encourage and also for putting up with me.

Chapter One

Two weeks back home in Sunset Ridge, Oklahoma, and Matthew Rivers found himself doing what he said he never would—drinking coffee at Chuck's Café and listening to the men at the table talk about small-town life. Not that he disliked Chuck and Jenni Stringer, or their café. He'd just hoped to avoid breakfast with his father and his friends as they discussed the world and how to fix it.

The conversation had started with cattle prices, moved on to their need for a pastor at Sonrise Community Church, and finally they discussed if the Jacksons' place would go up for sale now that Cliff Jackson had passed on and his kids had no interest in farming.

Matthew had only joined the morning crowd at Chuck's because he'd driven his dad, Buck Rivers—who'd run the gas out of his old farm truck—and it seemed Buck's day had no meaning if he didn't make it to breakfast with his friends. It was an odd bunch, this group. A retired lawyer, a bank president, a few local farmers, the mayor and Buck Rivers, Matthew's father.

It was more than likely that the men at this table had helped Buck out of a few scrapes.

The latest scrape was bigger than these men probably wanted to tackle. Buck was on the verge of foreclosure, and the property taxes hadn't been paid in two years.

Matthew had learned about the current set of problems to plague Buck and the Rocking R Ranch in a phone call. The call had come from Jenni Stringer, the same Jenni who wiped down tables and talked about the weather and gardening with her various customers. She'd explained to him, in her most maternal voice, that his dad's health seemed to be failing, and he might be on the verge of losing everything. It seemed, Jenni had said, that one of the boys ought to check on him.

Meaning Matthew should check on his father. Mark, Luke and Jonah sure wouldn't be showing up here to bail their father out. Their little sister, Jael, had never called the ranch home. His siblings had let him know that as the oldest, Matthew was responsible for Buck. And he was a pastor, they'd each reminded him. As if being a pastor made him more noble.

He hadn't filled them in on his current status. He'd taken a leave of absence from his ministry—the ministry he'd built from the ground up with his friend Jared Ellis.

He couldn't seem to come to grips with life and ministry without his best friend. He was no longer sure about his faith, about the calling or about his future. Six months ago, Jared had passed away. Taken from them by a virus that shouldn't have felled a strong, healthy man. A man of faith. A man with a heart for anyone hurting or in need.

Even now, Matthew felt the anger welling up inside

him. Would a true man of faith feel this much anger? Anger with God? For not answering his prayers? He was angry because Jared's wife of ten years had buried a man who was far better than Matthew. Better than most men. Angry because two little girls would grow up without their father.

He shook his head and focused on the half-empty cup of coffee he held between his hands. He listened to his dad tell a story about the work the two of them had done on the barn and then about the cattle they were thinking about buying. They. Father and son. Buck thought Matthew had returned for good.

He'd taken a leave of absence. He had six months to make decisions for his future and get Buck and the ranch back on track. He wasn't sure if the ranch could be profitable, not after decades of neglect.

Years ago, the Rivers ranch had been almost seven hundred acres of rolling fields, creek bottom land and some good stands of timber. Matthew's father had gambled away a big chunk to Jordan Pruitt and, over the years, had sold off more land just to keep the place going. That land he'd sold had been bought by none other than Cliff Jackson, the deceased neighbor whose offspring weren't interested in farming. And that was the crux of the issue. The Rivers brothers weren't that interested, either.

Maybe if Buck hadn't lost his mind drinking and gambling, the family wouldn't have scattered. Maybe their mother, Izzy, would have stayed and they might have had more than a passing relationship with their little sister, Jael. Maybe his brothers would be here, still working the ranch.

Buying it all back wouldn't change anything. Deep

down, he knew that. He knew the land wouldn't fix his parents, his brothers or even himself.

Matthew glanced at the front door as the bell jangled and a woman entered. She ducked her head, as if she didn't want to be noticed. He did notice.

She was average height with average brown hair, streaked with golden blond highlights. As she moved past him, she gave him a quick look, a surprised glance as their gazes clashed. Her eyes were not average. Her eyes were a beautiful, toffee brown, perfect for a golden complexion with strong but feminine features. Not that he noticed.

She hurried on past, the coral fabric of her dress whipping around her legs. She waved a greeting to an older woman sitting in the far corner of the café. That woman he did know. Sara Mitchell, church pianist. She had to be close to eighty.

Something about the younger woman tugged at memories from long ago. She seemed familiar. He knew her, but he couldn't place her. He'd been gone for eighteen years. He'd forgotten more people than he remembered.

He watched as Jenni Stringer filled coffee cups for both women and then returned to the dessert case to get whatever they'd ordered. The woman knew he was watching. Her cheeks turned a soft shade of pink and she wouldn't look his way. That brought a rare smile to his lips.

"Hey, Matthew." Brody Stringer, son of Chuck and Jenni, joined the men at their table, wiping his hands on his apron as he took a seat. "Did you know I got a new car?"

Matthew heard the question, but he'd gotten tangled up in trying to place the woman. He continued to glance her way, drawn to her, or maybe just trying to figure her out.

"Matthew, you aren't listening," Brody insisted as he scooted his chair closer to Matthew. Brody had been born with Down syndrome. His smile was contagious, his charm was legendary and his determination was second to none.

"You're right. I wasn't. I apologize." Matthew adjusted the brim of his cowboy hat and gave the younger man all of his attention.

Most of his attention. He stopped himself from staring at the woman and he gave Brody his full attention. "I'm listening. Promise."

"It's okay, Matthew. We have a Mustang. It's a hot rod. Dad let me drive it."

Chuck, retired marine and all muscle and brawn, paused mid-pour as he refilled coffee cups. "Hey, keep that quiet. You only drive that car on the back road to our house. Deputy John doesn't need to hear that you've been driving."

Brody laughed and his gray eyes sparkled with humor. "My dad is joking. Deputy John said I could drive on the back road because I'm a better driver than my mom."

"I imagine you are," Matthew agreed in a hushed tone. "I won't tell her you said that."

"I heard," Jenni called out from the counter where she was ringing up an order.

"She knows I am," Brody insisted. "Do you want to play a video game?"

"I'm going to have to leave, Brody, but I'll play the next time I'm in."

"Do you have work to do?" Brody asked.

"I do. I'm going to leave my dad and he'll get a ride home. Make sure he doesn't get in any trouble."

Brody gave him a steady look, then smiled. "No one keeps Buck out of trouble."

"I heard that," Buck Rivers said with a wink and a grin for Brody.

"I'm kidding, Mr. Rivers." Brody ducked his head, hiding his grin.

"I know you are," Buck answered.

Matthew studied the man who was his father and tried to piece together the Buck of today and the man who had raised him. This Buck smiled a little easier, lost his temper less often and took time for others. If only he'd shown up twenty years ago.

"Dad, if you're okay riding back with Mac," he said, mentioning a neighbor and the retired lawyer in the group, "I'm going on."

"Sounds like a plan."

"Brody, next time I'm here, we'll take that Mustang for a spin."

"Okay, Matthew." Brody twisted the towel he'd been holding and beamed at Matthew.

At the door, Matthew glanced back one last time, drawn again to the woman who had taken a seat at the back of the café.

He shrugged it off as he went out the door. It was perfect weather for late April. Not a cloud in the sky. His truck was on the opposite side of the street, facing the city park that took up space on the grassy square in the center of the downtown area. As he crossed to his truck, he heard the pitiful sound of a crying baby. He kept walking, because a crying baby wasn't unusual, even if it did sound close and he didn't see anyone in the area.

A bird might make a crying sound?

Except the sound didn't come from a bird. As he reached his truck, he heard it again, this time louder and more insistent. He searched the area, pushing back the brim of his cowboy hat to scan the playground.

The cry sputtered and mewed, strong and then weak, and it came from the bed of his truck. He spotted the infant carrier with a faded gray sun cover sitting next to his spare tire. A tiny face peered up at him, half-hidden by the enormous pacifier in its mouth. A faded and stained quilt covered the baby. A dirty backpack had been left on the tire.

"What in the world?" he murmured it quietly, not sure what else to say. "Where'd you come from?"

He heard car tires squeal and he spun to see if he could spot the vehicle before it sped away. He barely made out the back of the rusted-out blue sedan with no tags.

Matthew grabbed the handle of the carrier and lifted it from the back of his truck. He pulled back the sun cover so he could get a better look. Not the prettiest baby he'd ever seen, but definitely one of the tiniest.

Her skin seemed a bit yellow. Her weak cries grew louder and the distress turned her face red. Red and wrinkled. She also didn't smell too good.

"You need some help, don't you?" Matthew's experience with babies was limited to the occasional dedication he'd performed. Those babies had always been clean and dressed in frothy little outfits, their adoring parents holding them up for the entire congregation to catch a glimpse.

Pulling back the quilt that reeked of cat litter, he realized the infant wore only a little T-shirt with the words *Mommy's Girl* on the front.

Across the street, the door of the café opened. The mystery woman stepped out. She didn't appear to notice him, or maybe pretended she hadn't. He whistled and waved his free hand. She'd surely know how to help a baby.

She hesitated on the sidewalk.

"I need help over here," he shouted.

After several long seconds, she nodded and hurried across the street.

He was suddenly taken back in time. He was seventeen and the girl coming out of that café had been his best friend, Parker Smythe. Always smiling, always laughing. *Parker.* A little overweight, a lot smart and a person he thought he'd never see again. Until today. Coffee brown eyes with flecks of gold. That's what he'd noticed about the woman in the café—her eyes.

Parker's eyes.

Call her a coward, but the last person Parker Smythe wanted to see was Matthew Rivers. She didn't want to face him or the memory of their last conversation. At seventeen, the conversation had been heartbreaking in a way she hadn't expected. Even as a teenager, she'd been skilled at keeping her emotions in check. She'd been a pro at not getting too close to anyone. After all, her dad never pastored a church for more than three or four years. She'd learned early on that it hurt less if she kept friendships surface deep.

Matthew had been her big mistake.

She'd been back in town for over a week, and she'd

been doing a great job of avoiding him. Her work schedule, as a traveling nurse assigned to a nearby emergency room, meant long days.

She could no longer avoid him, not when he was standing there holding an infant seat and waving an arm at her. As she hurried across the street, she could hear a pitiful cry, the kind that got a woman right in the heart, and at her age—nearly thirty-five—the womb.

"What's wrong?" she asked as she hurried forward, not waiting, but taking the carrier from him. She pulled off the quilt and pushed the sun cover back. "Where did you find a baby in the five minutes since you left the café?"

The question bolted free, making her sound more like the teenager she'd been and not the woman she'd become. She should have known he'd have this effect over her.

"I'm just fortunate, I guess," he said it drolly, in a dry tone she would have recognized anywhere. *Even if he hadn't recognized her.* That thought came with a particularly nasty stab to her rather bruised heart.

"Someone left her in the back of my truck," he explained.

"What is this world coming to?" She repeated the phrase she'd often heard her parents say. That happened more and more as she got older and, maybe, as life left her a little on the jaded side. "We need to get her to the hospital."

"Right. I'm on that. I'm going to call 911." His voice had a catch in it that she felt to her soul. Who would leave their baby in the back of a truck? What kind of desperation pushed a mother to do such a thing?

Parker motioned for him to open the door of his

truck. "I'm guessing we can get her to Wagoner faster than an ambulance can get to us." She looked up and saw Jenni Stringer coming her way.

"What's going on? I heard Matthew calling for help."

Parker gave her a quick update and asked if she had any clean towels to wrap the child in. Jenni nodded and ran back to the café while Matthew waited for his call to click through.

He held the phone to his ear, a stunned look on his face as he glanced from her to the baby while responding to something that a dispatcher said to him. Probably along the lines of, "What's your emergency?"

"Someone abandoned an infant in the back of my truck." He paused. "Yes, you heard me right."

He glanced her way again. Ugh, those silvery gray eyes of his. Not just his eyes. All of him. He'd aged well. Couldn't he have gotten flabby? Maybe a rounded and less firm jawline? But no, his DNA won out and he was as handsome as ever, maybe more so.

It seemed best to ignore the look he was giving her. After Jenni returned with some towels, Parker wrapped the infant in the clean cloths, hefted her seat into the back and climbed in with the baby. Matthew gave her a questioning look and made no move to get behind the wheel and drive. The infant's condition was deteriorating. Her skin had a dusky look that didn't bode well, nor did the unsteady breaths that caused her stomach to collapse at each inhale and exhale.

"Matthew, we don't have time to waste here. Keep talking if you like, but get in this truck and drive." To Jenni, she said, "Thanks. We'll be in touch."

He opened the driver's side door as he continued his conversation with the 911 dispatcher, explaining the situation—the car he'd seen drive away. The woman on speaker asked about the baby's condition.

"Ma'am, I have no idea. I just know the baby is small and she needs help."

"Tell them that you have Parker Smythe with you. I'm an RN working at Wagoner. The infant is hours old, her breathing is shallow, her lips are blue. I'm guessing she weighs between three and four pounds and from the looks of the umbilical cord, it was a home delivery and not a good one. Now, let's drive. If they have a car in this vicinity, an escort would be nice."

"We can have an ambulance to you in thirty minutes," the dispatcher assured them.

Parker breathed through her frustration. It wasn't the dispatcher's fault, it was just the way things sometimes worked when a person lived miles from anywhere.

"And we can be at the hospital in fifteen. Tell them we don't have thirty minutes."

"We're leaving now," he told her and the dispatcher as he started his truck. "I'm glad to see you," he said, just to her, as he backed out of the parking space, his eyes meeting hers in the rearview mirror.

"I'm sure you are," she said, not meaning to be sarcastic. She guessed he might be glad to see her, considering the circumstances. Or maybe he truly was glad to see her, because they'd been friends until she messed things up.

Parker gave her full attention to the baby girl. "Pretty girl, this is a rough way to come into the world, isn't it?"

She stroked the thin strands of dark hair and prayed the baby would live. "Aren't you a pastor?" she asked. "Maybe you could pray."

He kept his eyes firmly on the road in front of him. “I don’t do a lot of praying these days.”

“Why?”

“I’m wondering if it works, and I don’t like leading folks on if it doesn’t.”

So he’d been hurt. That’s why he’d come home to a place he’d spent his teen years planning to escape. He’d only come home to lick his wounds. Fortunately, she didn’t have a moment to think about Matthew and whatever crisis had brought him back to Sunset Ridge.

“I’m sorry,” she said softly, glancing at his reflection in the mirror and then back to the baby girl. “She needs prayer.”

“She needs a miracle,” he muttered.

“That’s probably closer to the truth than anything else.” She leaned over, checking respirations, then pulse. “God bless you, little girl. Hang in there. You’re a tough cookie and I know you can do this. Just keep breathing.”

The speaker on his phone crackled. “How are you all doing,” the dispatcher asked.

“Driving,” Matthew answered.

Parker monitored pulse and breaths. She wished like anything that she had a pulse ox to check the infant’s oxygen levels.

“Is she okay?” Matthew asked.

“No. She isn’t okay at all. Just drive and if you still have that dispatcher, make sure she informed the hospital that our infant is in respiratory distress.” She felt fear welling up and she didn’t have time for that emotion. “Matthew, please pray.”

She leaned over the baby and started CPR. She gave her breath to the baby girl and she prayed. Even if he couldn't believe, she did. She'd believe enough for the both of them and for the infant fighting for her life.

And then she heard him. His prayer, his voice, both emotional and yet so soothing that she felt the peace of the words in her heart.

"Lord, if You're listening, please look over this little girl and hold her in the palm of Your hands. I'm not sure of the plan, but we have to trust. Let this baby receive a special touch from You and the help she needs at the hospital. May she always know that she is loved." He cleared his throat and she waited. "Amen."

Even if he hadn't wanted to pray and even if he didn't believe the words, it mattered. She'd needed the prayer as much as the baby girl.

She continued to help the baby breathe. She continued with miniscule chest compressions. Occasionally the tiny infant would respond with a breath of her own and a soft cry.

Matthew made brief comments to the dispatcher, who had not ended the call but remained on the line, every minute or so asking for an update. His voice was deeper, more mature, but still the voice of the teenager she'd known.

She'd been a fool to think he would ever love her. She'd always been the best friend. Even now, as a woman in her mid-thirties, men still saw her as the friend and not the woman they would date or marry.

She blamed herself. The constant moving as a child had caused her to create a shell around herself. She was happy, cheerful Parker, the best friend. Matthew had broken down her defenses with a hug, an arm around her shoulder and an understanding of her that no one else ever seemed to have.

Focus on the baby, she told herself, *not on the man behind the wheel of the truck.* They were hurtling through Wagoner and a patrol car had joined them, lights flashing and siren blaring as they navigated the traffic.

"We're almost there," she whispered to the tiny baby in her stained T-shirt. "I wonder where your mommy is and if she needs help."

"I'm sure she does," Matthew responded. "I hope she's okay."

At his words, she looked up and met his expression in the mirror before quickly refocusing on her patient. The last thing she needed was to soften toward him. The baby, on the other hand, deserved all of her attention.

Tomorrow they would go back to their normal, everyday lives, perhaps seeing each other from a distance or passing in the grocery store. She was only in town for a month or two, long enough to work and put more money in the bank, and then she would move on.

Matthew Rivers would once again be a memory.

Chapter Two

A group waited at the doors of the emergency room to the small, single-story hospital. Matthew wouldn't have guessed a hospital in Wagoner would even have a team available to meet them. As it turned out, they did and he took a deep and relieved breath at the sight.

He stopped his truck and the medical staff converged upon his vehicle. "We made it."

No answer.

Fear seized him and he glanced back at his passengers. She looked up, Parker, his once best friend. Her face had changed since high school, her cheekbones more defined, her eyes more somber, her hair lighter.

"She's okay?" he asked, afraid of the answer.

"She will be," Parker responded softly as she gathered up the infant, keeping her wrapped in the clean toweling that Jenni Stringer had provided. "She's so tiny."

"Let me get the door," he offered.

She nodded, her attention focused on the baby.

Matthew hurried to open the back door for her. She lifted her face, her eyes golden brown and searching, as if she, too, had recalled their last conversation. He felt the sting of it—his words, hers and the finality of hanging up and moving on without her in his life.

He pulled himself together and helped her from the truck, holding her arm as she slid to the ground, the baby whimpering in her arms.

And then he was forgotten, pushed to the side as the professionals rushed to take over. They questioned Parker and she gave short answers as they transferred the baby from her arms to the incubator. A nurse moved in with a manual resuscitator. She gently squeezed the bag and continued to do so as they hurried into the building, pushing the incubator.

Matthew, left behind by the busy crew, parked his truck and then went inside to find a seat in the waiting room. He picked through the pile of periodicals and found a conservation magazine. After that he flipped through dog-eared homemaking magazines with the recipes ripped out. The doors opened and he felt a rush of warm, outside air.

"How is she?" The voice, gruff and slightly strained, caught him by surprise.

He hadn't expected to see his father.

Buck took the seat next to Matthew, stretching his legs out and rubbing his knees in the process. Telltale signs of Buck's health issues.

"I'm not sure. No one has been out here to update me." Matthew glanced toward the doors of the ER, a move he'd made dozens of times since taking a seat. He glanced at his watch. An hour. He'd been sitting there for an hour and he wasn't sure why he hadn't gone on home.

Out of the corner of his eye, he saw Buck shift in his

seat. Matthew gave his dad another steady look, wondering about this man at his side, the same man who'd practically ignored that he had a family.

"How'd you get here?" Matthew asked.

"Jenni Stringer and Brody. They're parking the car. Jenni says that until a parent shows up, if they show up, that baby girl belongs to the town."

"She needs to belong to someone," Matthew said, thinking about the baby left like yesterday's garbage in the back of his truck.

The doors opened again and Jenni and Brody joined them on the uncomfortable plastic covered seats.

"Any news?" Jenni asked as she took the seat next to Buck.

"None."

Brody had taken the spot next to Matthew and it brought back memories of how he was always at the Rivers boys' side. They'd been teenagers and Brody was just a little guy with a wide grin and empathy that continually took them by surprise. He'd always seemed to know when they needed a friend. Even if the friend was a dozen years younger and sometimes overlooked.

"She'll be okay, Matthew." Brody leaned close. "I prayed all the way here."

"Thanks, Brody." Matthew rested a hand on the younger man's shoulder.

Brody grinned. "I prayed for the baby and our lives. Have you ridden with my mom?"

Matthew felt the tension inside him ease. "Brody, I'm glad you're here."

A short time later, Parker joined them. He stood. She avoided looking at him. He didn't blame her. A lifetime ago they'd been best friends and then she'd called him that first semester of college and confessed that she loved him. It had taken him by surprise and, being a stupid teenager, he probably hadn't handled it with a lot of sensitivity.

Regrets ate him up and he wished he could take it back, for the girl she'd been and this woman who seemed more confident, but not quite ready for a reunion.

"Looks like we have a big support system for our little girl," Parker stated as she took in the four of them.

"We wanted that for her," Jenni said. "How is she?"

Matthew stepped back, giving Parker room and allowing her to include them all in the conversation. He just wished she'd get on with it. The worry was gnawing at him and it managed to get tangled up with memories of the days he'd spent visiting Jared.

"She's small, very small, and newborn."

"Will she be okay?" Matthew asked.

"I think she will. You know I can't give a lot of specifics. There are privacy laws."

"And we're not her family," Buck muttered. "But it seems to me, she needs a family."

"She does," Parker agreed.

Matthew saw the moisture gather in her eyes. She quickly blinked it away. "I'm glad you could tell us she's going to be okay," Matthew said.

"Me, too." Parker put a hand to her neck and rubbed. "I'm afraid that's all I have for now. She'll be in the nursery, and if needed, they'll transfer her to a bigger hospital."

"Thank you," Matthew started and then hesitated. What else could he say? "If it's okay, I'll stick around."

"I'm sure that's fine. The police are here and they'll

be taking statements. I'm going back in and I'll let them know that you're waiting."

He nodded, words seeming useless. Parker left and he returned to his seat. Brody picked up a magazine and flipped through it, exclaiming over the cool muscle cars. Matthew's dad had closed his eyes and was either dozing or praying.

"I'm going to take a walk down the hall," he said to no one in particular. "Anyone need anything?"

"We'll be fine here," Jenni assured him.

Matthew left the waiting room and walked down the hall. The hospital had fewer than twenty rooms and all were on the ground floor. At the end of the main hall, he could go left to the nursery and obstetrics or right. He took the right and saw a sign that indicated one of the rooms to be a chapel.

The word chapel might have been a bit of an exaggeration. The small room held a bench facing a table with a Bible, a lamp and several candles. Four chairs were lined up midway back from the bench and a rocking chair in the corner sat next to a table with another Bible that had been left open to the book of Psalms. He took a seat, unable to ignore the sense of peace he felt in that makeshift sanctuary.

Even a jaded minister could forget his bitterness for a few moments of quiet, and he could put the baby first, thinking about her, her fragile health and the mother who had been desperate enough to abandon her.

Matthew hadn't given the mother much thought until that moment, except to judge her for what appeared to be very callous actions. Now, given time to think about it, he wondered about her. He wondered if she was safe, if she needed help as desperately as her baby had needed help.

He bowed his head to pray, even if he wasn't sure how his prayers would be received. He hadn't prayed much since Jared's death. He had spent the past six months doubting everything he'd ever believed or taught, including his faith, and wondering why his prayers hadn't been answered.

He opened his eyes, looked up and noticed the painting of Jesus that hung above the table where the Bible rested on a stand and the lamp glowed with soft light.

"Now here I sit, once again asking You to hear my prayers, and I'm not even sure if I believe You're listening," he whispered into the stillness, his words taking the peace of the room and shattering it.

"That was at least an honest prayer," a voice said.

He turned, not really expecting God, but feeling as if now would be the moment that God would arrive to rebuke his unbelief. Instead, it was an older gentleman in a faded gray suit, a worn, well-used Bible tucked under his arm.

"I'm sorry to interrupt," the gentleman said. "I'm George Rogers, chaplain."

Matthew came to his feet to shake the hand George extended.

"Matthew Rivers," Matthew answered, ashamed because he wished he still had this room to himself. Also, ashamed that this man had heard his angry words at the God they both served.

"Can I help you, Matthew?" George Rogers had the kindest, easiest voice Matthew had ever heard. A radio voice. A pastor voice. The kind that probably reverberated through a congregation, filling them with wonder as he preached sermons he never doubted.

"No," Matthew answered. "I'm just waiting for news on the infant we brought in."

"The Jane Doe. The police are here. You must be the witness they're searching for."

"I would guess I probably am," Matthew said. "I should go." Strangely, he didn't want to walk away from the chaplain.

"Matthew, I'm not God's spokesman or His defender. Well, perhaps I am. Sometimes age gives one wisdom. Also, the ability to say things that others won't." Chaplain Rogers smiled to punctuate his words. "He's listening. Maybe the answer isn't always what we ask for or even want, but the answers will someday make sense. Sometimes the miracle is the thing we least expect or even asked for."

Matthew nodded and started to walk away, but he couldn't. He knew that Chaplain Rogers wasn't a mind reader, but how had he known Matthew's struggles, his doubts?

"Chaplain Rogers, if you would pray for that little girl, for the Jane Doe, I would appreciate that."

A hand, strong but as worn as the Bible he carried, touched Matthew's shoulder. Matthew felt that in that moment, George Rogers also said a prayer for him.

"I'll pray."

Matthew left the room. He'd known some good pastors, decent men. A few minutes in George Rogers's presence and he knew that George was the real deal, a man who lived and preached his very genuine faith. He probably didn't minister to large congregations and probably wasn't well-known. He was the humble kind of pastor who quietly served without recognition.

Had he ever been that man, Matthew wondered? Or had he been a charlatan, a man who slid into a career because he found it came easy to him? He'd beaten himself up with the verse that said the effectual fervent prayer of a righteous man availeth much. Maybe he wasn't the righteous man who ought to be praying for others.

The police presence at the end of the hall drew him. He knew he would find the baby there, and Parker.

Parker.

They'd shared a lot of secrets, a lot of dreams back in the day. He hated that he'd hurt her. He'd been a thoughtless teenager and he hadn't understood what it took for her to tell him how she felt.

At that moment she entered the hall. Her soulful toffee eyes sought him out. She smiled, the way she'd smiled years ago, seeming happy to see him. For a moment, they were friends again. Until they weren't. Until the look changed as she remembered.

She nodded in his direction and the police officer motioned for him to join them.

"Mr. Rivers, we're writing up our report on the infant Jane Doe. Is it possible you have a connection to the baby?"

"Connection?" he asked. "Other than finding her in the bed of my truck?"

"Is it possible…?" The officer cleared his throat and a splash of red colored his youthful cheeks. "Could you be the infant's father?"

He nearly laughed but he sobered and answered. "I'm not the baby's father."

The officer looked down at the tablet he typed his

notes into. “Do you know the mother, or father? Did you see anything suspicious as you left the café?”

“I do not know the parents and, as I told the dispatcher, I saw a rusted-out, blue sedan leaving the square. No plates.”

“It takes a different kind of person to do this to a baby,” one of the officers said as they finished their questions.

“We don’t know her situation,” Parker defended.

Matthew agreed. “We don’t know what drove her to take such a desperate measure. I think we should show mercy. You might have two victims—the baby and the mother.”

The older of the officers nodded slowly in agreement. His name tag said William Baxter. “We’ll let you all know if we learn anything regarding the Jane Doe, or her mother.”

“Faith,” Matthew said.

“I’m sorry? What?” Officer Baxter’s eyebrows drew together.

“Her name is Faith. She deserves to be more than a Jane Doe.”

The man touched a finger to his forehead in an informal salute. “Noted.”

They left and he was alone with Parker.

“Do you want to see her?” she asked.

“I think I’ll head home.”

Her head tilted to one side. “You can’t leave, you’re my ride back to Sunset Ridge. Come in and tell her good-bye.”

Parker didn’t give him a chance to make an excuse. Her hand circled his wrist and she took him through the double doors and into the world he’d rather avoid—the world of monitors, respirators and hopeful prayers.

The Wagoner hospital was smaller than most and there were only a few babies. The little girl he'd impulsively named Faith rested in an incubator. Tubes and wires attached to monitors. Her little hands and feet clenched and kicked.

"What an awful way to enter the world and life." Matthew rested a hand on the incubator. "I wish you well, Faith."

"Pray they find her a home. The caseworker said they're short on foster homes, as usual. She asked if one of us would take her."

"That's pretty desperate," he agreed. "At least if they're thinking I would take her. I think you're a much better candidate."

"Because I'm a woman?" she asked with a hint of teasing in her tone. "I'm not a good candidate. I'm a traveling nurse with no home of my own. I won't be staying in Oklahoma. You're probably more qualified than you think."

"She's small." He changed the subject with that observation.

"She was born early, but they think also malnourished in the womb. She has some other small battles to fight."

"That you can't share with me."

Her mouth curved into that generous smile he remembered well. She'd always been beautiful, but she hadn't believed that about herself. She'd only ever seen her weight and she'd let that define who she was.

"I can't," she said. "In any other situation we wouldn't be talking about her at all, but since you found her..."

"You also found her." He gave her a quick grin. "We're in this together, just like old times."

"Not at all like old times, Matthew."

She was right. They were no longer the kids they'd been. She'd been the new girl, pastor's daughter, moving from place to place every few years and using her outgoing personality to ease herself into new situations. He'd been the oldest of the four Rivers brothers, which had been enough of a stigma for most parents to keep their daughters away from him. No matter that he'd played basketball, studied hard and earned a scholarship, he was still a Rivers.

"Not old times," he agreed softly. "Or even the people we once were. I just hope this little girl can grow up strong and healthy." Better to keep it about the baby. "And maybe you can give me an update from time to time."

"She's a fighter. She'll make it just fine and we can pray for the right home. And I'll keep you updated."

He stood next to the incubator and swallowed fear for the tiny baby girl that he'd named Faith. He studied her scrunched up little face, and then he heaved a sigh when she opened her eyes and looked up at him. Her eyes were so dark in her tiny face.

Trust. The baby girl, abandoned at birth, looked at him with trust. He couldn't fathom it. Somehow Parker's hand slipped into his and they stood there together.

She would leave in a matter of weeks, she'd said. It wasn't really enough time to get to know each other again. She didn't seem to want to spend time with him.

That was probably for the best.

Parker had to get her act and her emotions, together. She'd known when she took this position that she might see Matthew again. She'd spent the time since they'd arrived at the hospital telling herself it didn't matter. He didn't matter. She was no longer the overweight teenager who had given him her heart.

She would be thirty-five in the fall. She had a job she loved. She even loved herself. That was saying something. She'd spent her teen years pretending at self-acceptance, pretending it didn't hurt when she was teased. Or worse, ignored and left out.

Matthew had, in a way, been the catalyst for her healthier self. When he'd laughed and told her that it was nothing personal, but she was wasting her time on a guy who would never get married, she'd taken it personally. She'd stopped eating her emotions. She'd started exercising and eating healthy. She'd lost weight.

She would never be thin. She smiled at that realization. She loved food too much to be thin. She disliked exercise too much.

As she stood next to Matthew, watching as he touched baby Faith's little hand, she admitted that the years had been good to him. He was taller, broader and even better looking than the wiry boy she'd known.

The thin face of a teen had filled out to become the handsome face of a man. His hair, longer as a teen, was now cut short and had hints of silver at the temples. He smelled good, too. Soap, coffee and an expensive cologne he hadn't worn as a teenager. Back then it had been body spray from a can. This hinted at dark forests and mountain air.

Her heart did a silly, familiar dance. That reaction belonged to the teenage Parker, not the woman. She stepped away from him to watch as Dr. Finley entered the room to check on their patient.

He smiled as he gave her a careful examination. He adjusted the nasal cannula that was too large for her tiny face.

"Her color is better. And that bath certainly made her more pleasant," Dr. Finley said as he leaned to listen to Faith's chest. When he straightened, he let out a long and troubled sigh and watched the monitor. "Seems stable for the moment. When she first came in, I was more concerned, but her heart rate and BP have leveled out."

"Poor baby girl. It's a rough way to start life." Parker blinked away the tears that fogged her vision. "I hope we can keep her here with us."

"If she remains stable, that's a possibility." Dr. Finley scratched at the back of his neck. "I hope they can find a good placement for her. That is, if they can't put her with family."

"What have we got here?" the charge nurse coming on for her shift asked. "Is this our Jane Doe?"

"She isn't a Jane," Matthew said with a warning tone.

"And you are?" Nurse Martin asked.

"The man who found her. And her name is Faith."

"Faith, is it?" Nurse Martin raised a brow as she inspected the flow of the IV line connected to Faith's tiny arm. "I think that's a perfect name. She's going to need some faith."

The monitors began to beep. Dr. Finley stepped back to the incubator. Parker hit the reset button on the machine and Nurse Martin pushed her way in to help.

"What's going on?" Matthew asked.

"Her heart rate is dropping and her blood oxygen levels are low," Parker explained. She ignored that firm line of his mouth. She didn't have the time to make him feel better about the situation. Faith needed all hands on deck.

"We're going to intubate." Dr. Finley nodded to Nurse Martin.

"Sir, if you're not family or a guardian, you're going to need to leave."

Matthew leaned in. "I'm the man who found this baby in my truck. At this point she obviously doesn't have family."

"I'm going to have to ask you to leave," Dr. Finley repeated.

"I—" he started.

Parker took him by the hand and led him to the door. "You can wait, but you can't be in here. I'll be with her."

He grazed her with a look, but his focus shot to the baby as Dr. Finley and the nurse worked to stabilize their patient.

"Keep her safe," he said, his voice hoarse.

She gave his hand a quick squeeze. "I'll do everything I can."

She stepped back from him and shut the door, closing him out of the room. When she turned, Dr. Finley had the tubing in. He might not be a pediatric specialist, but she felt better with him in the room. Nurse Martin's experience also couldn't be ignored. She handled everything as Dr. Finley called out instructions.

Parker stayed next to the incubator, ready to help if they needed her and praying Faith's little body could withstand the trauma of her birth. For a moment she let her eyes slide shut and she prayed. As she did, she also prayed for Matthew, for whatever had brought him home, whatever it was that made him so somber.

A lab technician entered through the glass door. "We

got the results on her labs. I thought I'd run it down here so you wouldn't have to wait."

Dr. Finley pulled on his glasses and looked over the tablet the lab worker handed him. "Not surprised that mom was using drugs. At least we know what we're dealing with and we've already got her on antibiotics to fight that infection."

Parker's heart sank, knowing that Faith could possibly face a lifetime of challenges due to the choices her mother had made.

"Who does this?" Parker said it to the room in general, knowing none of them had answers.

"Someone desperate and using," Nurse Martin muttered. "Hopefully the mom is alive."

"I hadn't thought of that," Parker said as she soothed the crying baby girl. "Oh, sweet Faith, we will take care of you."

"That name will stick," Dr. Finley said as he leaned in to listen to Faith's heart and lungs. "I'm sorry for this, little peanut. What a day you've had."

The baby's mouth opened in a silent cry.

What a day, indeed. At least the parents had put her in the right place and with the right person. Had that been on purpose or just a fortunate coincidence?

They all watched the monitors, watched the heart rate begin to stabilize and oxygen levels increase. Crisis over, but there would probably be more hills to climb for their little patient. A lifetime of hills, if the drugs had done the likely damage often seen in drug addicted babies.

Unable to stem the tears that had started to fall, Parker left the room. She didn't want to talk. She didn't want to discuss why this hurt so much. She wanted to find a place to pray and to cry.

She picked the wrong room. As she entered the normally empty chapel, she saw him there. Matthew sat on a bench, leaning slightly forward, his head bowed. He straightened and looked up as she entered and he nodded.

"Is she okay?" he asked, his voice gruff with emotion.

"She will be," she answered. "In time."

"You okay?" he asked.

"I will be," she gave the duplicate answer. "In time."

He moved over, making room for her to sit next to him on the narrow bench facing a painting of Jesus. It was the last place she wanted to be and the only place she wanted to be.

"Were you praying?" She whispered the question.

"*The effectual fervent prayer of a righteous man availeth much.* I don't think I'm effectual, fervent or righteous. So you tell me. Does God listen to my prayers if I doubt my faith?"

"I'm not sure if you doubt as much as you think. You're here."

He gave a humorless laugh. "I don't know about that. I'm pretty angry with God and with myself."

"You're human, Matthew."

This wasn't the conversation she wanted to have with him. It went too deeply into his personal life, which was the last place she wanted or needed to be.

And then his hand touched hers. His fingers slipped between her fingers. She closed her eyes against the way it felt to have him hold her hand again.

"I have one prayer," he said. "Just, save her. Please. I don't have the faith to move mountains. I don't have the faith…" His free hand went to his eyes. "I want that little girl to live."

"I don't think it was an accident that she was placed in the back of your truck," Parker told him. He might not want to hear it, but she believed and she felt that God had a plan in all of this. "God knew exactly where she needed to be."

"Last year I probably would have agreed with you. Today, I'm holding out hope, and believe me, hope and I are at odds right now."

"Could be that this baby, Faith, is a lesson for us both. We can't change the outcome of her situation, but we can have faith, we can hope, we can pray."

"We can pray." He released her hand and stood. "I should get you back to town. Jenni took my dad back to the farm, but I need to get back there and make sure he's staying out of trouble."

"How is he?" she asked.

"Sober for the first time in years. Aging faster than he should." He shrugged. "Better than he's probably been in my lifetime."

They stopped by the nursery on their way out of the building. Matthew's eyes closed as he stood by the incubator, his hand touching the top of the enclosure. "Be safe, little Faith," he whispered before turning to go.

"I'm sure they'll let you visit her," Parker told him as they walked out of the building.

He shook his head. "I don't think so."

The refusal bothered her. He cared. She knew he cared. So why would he not want to visit? Because it was too hard? As if it wasn't hard for that little girl to be abandoned and then struggle to survive. She had so many things she wanted to say to him as anger and impatience bubbled up.

Years ago, she would have said what was on her mind.

As they got in his truck to leave, she said only one thing. Probably the worst thing she could have said. "It's easy for you to walk away. As if she doesn't matter."

She immediately wanted to groan, and possibly run away. What a silly, rotten thing to say to him.

He jerked his head toward her, a look of shock and hurt in his eyes, before they went carefully blank. "And here I thought we were going to be friends again."

She ignored him, because she didn't want the truth between them. It would be easy to fall back into friendship with Matthew. But friendship wasn't what she wanted and she was tired of the "best friend" role in the lives of the men she knew. Her last "best friend" had proposed to a co-worker and asked her to be his best man at their wedding.

She was done being the friend. She'd been described with every sunny, happy, joyful adjective in the book. The words that always hurt were the ones that started with, "just a little overweight." She'd made a discovery in the last few years. She liked herself. She liked the person God had created and that person was more than hair, makeup, clothing and the number on her digital scale. The person on the inside mattered. Her happiness mattered. She wouldn't let a man steal that from her. She wouldn't give Matthew Rivers the opportunity.

Even though he hadn't really asked.

Chapter Three

Matthew glanced at the woman sitting next to him in his truck. They had a fifteen-minute drive to Sunset Ridge. This time, without a baby to care for, silence hung heavy between them.

It wasn't an easy, friendly silence. More the kind that grew and felt as thick as cotton surrounding them. Parker kept her focus on the window. He reached to turn up a classic George Strait song that played on the country station.

"I hope she'll be okay," he said after a few minutes of the heavy and uncomfortable silence.

"Me, too." She let out a trembly sigh. "We can pray. And also, there are good doctors and nurses caring for her. I hope they find her mom."

"Yeah." He didn't know what else to say. He did know that he wanted to move on to an easier topic.

"Traveling nurse, huh?" He gave her a quick grin. "I always thought you would settle down and have a family and never move again. You hated moving."

"Yeah, I did. This is different, though. I'm seeing new places other than Sunset Ridge. In June I'm going to Destin, Florida, and I'm living in a beachfront condo for a couple of months. I've always wanted to live on the coast. Not forever, but for a bit."

"What's the end goal?"

She gave him a quick glance. "A place of my own. One that I'll have forever. Maybe a horse or two, a garden, a dog."

"That sounds good," he acknowledged. "You're staying in town while you're here?"

"Yes. The hospital rents rooms from Erma Adams."

"We should have lunch."

The sharp look she gave him told him what she thought of the idea.

"Or not," he mumbled.

"I think not."

He pulled in next to her car and she sat there a moment, as if getting her bearings. She'd been so composed with baby Faith. She'd known exactly what to do. That self-assurance had disappeared.

"You hurt me," she admitted with a gentle smile. "We were best friends and you really hurt me. I was a teenager who pretended to have self-esteem and you made me feel like nothing."

"I'm sorry. I was a stupid teenager and you really were my best friend. Why ruin a good friendship?"

"Right," she said. He got the impression she wasn't convinced.

Not giving her a chance to object, he got out and hurried to her side of the truck to open the door.

"This isn't necessary," she told him as she climbed down. "But thank you."

He gave her a grin and chivalrous tip of his hat. He'd always been too serious, because that's what his teen years demanded. But he did, occasionally, know how to be charming.

"It isn't going to work," she informed him.

He saw the quick flash of humor she tried to hide. Her eyes—always expressive, full of emotion and light—twinkled. He gave her a knowing look that she ignored.

"I have to go," she told him as she reached for her car door. He beat her to it and pulled it open.

"Same. I need to get back to the ranch. Buck left to his own devices is never a good thing."

"No, probably not." She swung her keys in her hand. "Whoever the parents are, I'm glad they picked your truck."

"I'm glad they picked my truck when you were nearby to help."

She gave a quick nod. Then she was in her car and the door closed, a definite signal that the reunion had ended.

Matthew climbed back in his truck. For a long moment he sat there, staring at the little park in the center of the town square. Sunset Ridge, as close to Mayberry as a person could get. And yet, today someone had decided to toss away a baby girl. Why?

He might have taken a break from ministry, maybe he'd never go back, but he couldn't stop caring about people. Somewhere out there a mom, maybe two parents, felt they had no options but to leave their baby behind. It made his heart ache thinking about that mom, probably young and probably thinking she had nowhere to turn.

He started his truck and backed out of the parking space, catching sight of a family just arriving, their children running to the swings and a dog on a leash tugging to catch up. They appeared to be the kind of family that every child should be a part of. Would Faith become a part of a family that took their dog to the park? The kind of family with a dad who carried her on his shoulders and a mom who pushed her on the swing?

For the first time in his life, he wondered what kind of father he might have been, had he married and if he'd been a dad. Mid-thirties and he'd never allowed himself to think of himself in terms of fatherhood or even being a husband. He'd been content with ministry, with his life in Chicago.

He'd spent a lifetime afraid of becoming his father. He'd spent his adult years worrying that if he ever became a father, he'd let his children down in some way. The way Buck and Izzy had let their children down.

Matthew headed back to the ranch, once gloriously called the Rocking R. The arch over the driveway was rusted and leaned a bit to the left. The sign, like the ranch, had seen better days. The place was in shambles, from the overgrown pasture to the barn and even the two-story farmhouse that had been a showplace in the days of his grandparents.

He pulled past the house and parked in front of the barn. Buck, hat pulled low, glanced up from hammering a length of treated lumber to a post in an effort to repair the corral. A nosy cow stood nearby, probably wondering what in the world Buck was doing patching up her escape route. As Matthew got out of his truck, his dad straightened and pushed back the cowboy hat he'd been wearing for too many years.

Matthew should buy his father a new hat. He would add it to the list of things to get. Fencing, posts, roofing for the barn, shingles for the house and maybe a couple of good horses. Horses always seemed to make a place a little better.

"I guess Jenni brought you home?" Matthew asked. "I'm sorry for leaving you on your own. The police showed up."

"Yeah, the police talked to us, too. Jenni took me back to town and planned on driving me out here, but Sam Thompson was at the café with a couple of church deacons and he offered to drive me home."

It might have been the look Buck gave him, or maybe something in his tone, but Matthew got the feeling he should walk away from whatever conversation he was about to be a part of.

"Don't get that look on your face," Buck said. "They know you're too high in the instep for a little church like Sunset Ridge Community. They thought maybe you'd fill in some Sunday. They haven't been able to get a pastor for four years so they have guest speakers or one of the members will bring a lesson."

"Why can't they get a minister?" Matthew asked, regretting the question. He didn't want his father getting ideas. Ideas that he would stay, or even worse, take on the role of pastor in the local church. Local congregations were tough. They knew too much about his life. Not that he'd be interested in staying here, pastoring here.

"No one wants the little churches," Buck answered with a thoughtful look. "Not enough glory or money in it."

"Dad, I'm not preaching. I'm not even sure if I'm going back to my church."

"Now that don't make a lick of sense," Buck said.

"What happened to you? From what I saw on those online videos, you were doing mighty fine up there."

His dad had watched his sermons? He didn't know how to process that revelation. He could imagine his dad at the decades-old dining room table, watching his son's sermons on the laptop his daughter Jael had bought and showed him how to use. If Matthew had to guess, Buck probably talked to the screen and pointed out anything he didn't agree with.

"I guess I just need a break," he explained to Buck. "Let's get started on these corrals. I've chased more cows back in than I ever wanted to in my life."

"I can't quite figure you out," Buck said. "I guess you aren't going to talk about what you're running from. At least not with me. Maybe I haven't earned that right."

"Dad, it isn't about you or what you have or haven't earned. I'm here. For now, this is where I want to be. I want to be here."

"Building fences."

"Not chasing cattle."

"Well?" Buck asked, as he leaned to grab another nail. "What about that baby?"

"She'll live," Matthew said as he held the board in place. "Hopefully."

"What about that little gal, Parker?"

"She'll live, too." He hedged, knowing that wasn't what Buck meant.

"Don't try that on me. The two of you were friends, but I'm guessing you haven't seen her since you went off to college."

There were accusations in that statement, or maybe Matthew felt guilty. He glanced at his dad, but Buck kept working, never losing the toothpick he held between his teeth. He hammered a nail in place and checked to make sure the board didn't need another.

The farm dog, a Border collie mix named Pete, jumped to chase a rabbit. Buck whistled and the dog trotted back and sat, waiting expectantly for a treat. Buck pulled a piece of bacon out of his pocket and tossed it for the dog to catch.

Buck gave him another look, and this one obviously meant that he expected some kind of answer regarding Parker. It took him a minute to find it, and to get past his father's weathered gaze. Buck had aged. His craggy face was heavily lined. His skin, always tan from working outside, was on the leathery side. He hadn't shaved in days and his hair had gone mostly gray.

"You're right, it is the first time I've seen her since I left for college. It seemed better that way."

"Because she had a crush on you?"

Matthew would have denied it, but it seemed it had been the truth. He'd never forget the phone call and how it had sent him into a tailspin, wondering how he'd led her on. That had never been his intention.

"Yeah," he responded, wishing they weren't having this conversation.

"I tried to warn you." Buck pried another worn and busted board loose.

Matthew grabbed the length of treated lumber that would replace it.

It had been some years, but he remembered the conversation that had taken place just months before his graduation from high school. Buck hadn't been sober when he'd accused Matthew of leading that little church girl on, making her think he liked her. Maybe if Matthew's father hadn't been drinking, or maybe if he'd ever given solid advice or taken on a real parental role, then Matthew would have listened and shown a little more respect. Instead, he'd told his father to stay out of his business.

"Yeah, you did try to warn me."

"Don't beat yourself up. You were a kid," Buck offered with a thump on Matthew's back. The camaraderie fit about as well as a pair of too small shoes.

"I never meant to hurt her," he admitted.

"None of us ever mean to hurt the people we care about," Buck said. And then he cleared his throat, shoved his hat down on his head and went to grab more lumber.

Matthew guessed that might be the closest his father had ever come to apologizing to his sons. He hadn't come home expecting apologies, forgiveness or a big family reunion. He'd come home to escape his life for a little while, deal with his anger and be a son who took care of his father when his father needed help.

An image of Parker flashed through his mind. He hadn't expected to see her or to face the way he'd hurt her. He'd let it go and he'd forgotten. She obviously hadn't forgotten. At the very least, he needed to ask forgiveness before she left.

The next afternoon, Parker walked out of a patient's room, washed her hands and met the gaze of a visitor, a woman standing near the nurse's station. Parker smiled as she passed by the other woman. She could clock out in fifteen minutes. She wanted to get through her shift and then visit Faith.

After checking on a patient in one of the exam rooms,

she returned to the nurse's station. "Anything else, John?" she asked the PA.

John, charming, forty and divorced, looked up from the computer screen and winked at her. "Dinner."

"Nope."

"I'm not giving up," he said.

"You should," she countered.

She'd been here for a little more than two weeks and he'd played this game every day since week one. She didn't date co-workers. It never worked out. At least it didn't for her. She preferred to come in, do her job and then, when the contract ended, move to the next hospital. Being a traveling nurse had the benefit of keeping her moving. Which seemed ironic since as a child, she hated the moving, just as Matthew had pointed out. Her pastor father constantly moved his family from one small and broken church to another.

He'd kept them in Sunset Ridge for five years, the longest they ever lived in one place. It gave her the opportunity to go to high school and not move and change friends.

Five years of not moving, not having to make new friends, not pretending she was always happy and that the teasing about her weight didn't bother her. Five years of being best friends with Matthew Rivers.

Five unfortunate years of falling in love.

Ugh, that was so pitiful. She brushed it off, smiled at their visitor and went to clock out. That's when the visitor decided to make herself known.

"Parker Smythe?" the woman called out, following her down the hall to the locker room.

Parker stopped, smiling as she waited. "Yes."

"I'm Jackie Peterson. I'm going to be our Jane Doe's caseworker."

"Faith," Parker informed the woman. "She deserves a name."

"You're right, she does. Can I walk with you?"

"Of course."

"She's going to need a foster home," Jackie Peterson said as they walked. "Someone with nursing experience."

Oh, now she understood. "I'm not the person."

"You could be." Jackie grinned. "We're so short on homes willing to take these little babies. Actually, we're short on homes. Period."

"I know it's a problem. My parents were foster parents for several years." And Parker had gone through the certification process herself but had not fostered a child yet.

"So you're already experienced."

At that, Parker laughed. "Good try. I'm not the person. I live in a rented room in Sunset Ridge. I'm leaving in a month."

"Maybe a temporary placement."

"I work long hours."

"The hospital has day care on-site."

Another little round of laughter, although Parker felt far from amused.

"You're determined," Parker told the other woman. "I don't feel like I'm the best person. I love visiting her, but I'm an unmarried woman, living in one room and moving in a month. She needs a home, a family, two parents and stability."

"But you love her and that means a lot—I was told how good you were with her."

"Maybe it does, but…"

"Pray about it."

They'd stopped walking as they came to the doors to the obstetrics wing, where the nursery was located. Parker closed her eyes, just briefly, as she stood in the hallway.

"That's unfair." Asking her to pray when she'd done nothing but pray. Prayer didn't change the reality of her situation.

"I'm sorry. Desperate times and all that." Jackie touched her arm. "Think about it. We have a week or two before she's released."

"I'll think about it. It couldn't be permanent and I just feel the less she has to move from place to place, the better."

"Even a temporary home helps, Parker. It gives us the opportunity to find a permanent home."

Parker nodded and then she pushed the button on the intercom.

"We'll be in touch," Jackie assured her as a farewell.

Parker knew the caseworker wouldn't give up and she understood why she felt the determination to place Faith. If Parker's situation had been different, she would have loved to take the little girl into her home and give her a loving start in life.

A stab of something like grief hit her heart. Like most women, she'd wanted a husband, babies and the home with the white picket fence. As a girl, she had scribbled names in notebooks, played games that told her the name of the man she might marry and even plucked petals off daisies. As if daisies predicted love.

She'd prayed. For years she'd prayed that God would guide her, that He would send the man who would love her and be a part of her life. As much as she wanted to marry and have children, she didn't want to marry outside of God's will for her life.

So here she was, almost thirty-five, single and wondering where her answers to those prayers might be.

She was buzzed into the obstetrics wing, and as she walked down the hall in the direction of the nursery, she saw a commotion. The type of commotion that meant someone might be in the midst of a medical emergency. She picked up her pace, hurrying toward the glass-walled room. She pushed the door open and was greeted by high pitched alarms and a flurry of activity.

Dr. Finley looked up from the incubator and then he went back to work, giving directions to the nurse on duty. Hazel, Parker thought might have been her name. The nurse glanced her way, a worried frown marring her features.

"What happened?" Parker asked as she joined them.

Faith, tiny but a mighty little warrior, fought against the hands that examined her. Tiny little fingers grabbed, and silent cries turned her face red.

"She's a sick little girl," Dr. Finley said as he moved the stethoscope from lungs to abdomen. "Where do you want to start? Withdrawal, infection, a heart murmur and bradycardia."

"Does she need to be moved?" Parker asked as she washed her hands.

"I'd rather not put her through the stress of the move unless we have to." Dr. Finley studied the monitors for a moment. "Give me a few minutes and we'll get the room warmed up so you can hold her. I always believe that touch is an important medicine for these little ones."

"I can hold her?" Parker asked in disbelief.

"You're the closest she has to a mother, Parker. She needs you."

The closest Faith had to a mother. The words sank into her heart.

She swallowed, afraid that if she spoke, she would be reduced to tears. Not just tears, ugly crying with sobs and those after-crying hiccups. This baby had won her heart in a way that left her frightened and vulnerable.

"I need to make a phone call," she whispered as she hurried from the room, confused and needing guidance, reassurance…friendship.

A phone call to Matthew. Seventeen years and she needed him all over again, as if they'd never stopped being friends, as if he hadn't broken her heart. As if he could still be the first person she called when she needed to tell someone whatever might be on her mind or heart.

He hadn't meant to hurt her or break her heart, she reminded herself. Matthew had been honest. That's all he'd ever been with her. She dialed the number he'd given her the previous day.

After several rings, he answered. "Matthew Rivers."

She opened her mouth to speak but the sob broke free from the tightness of her throat and tears slid down her cheeks.

"Parker?"

She nodded, wiping at her eyes and breathing through what felt like hysteria. She'd been the nurse at so many bedsides, witnessing the distress of a family member over a sick loved one.

Baby Faith wasn't her loved one, but she deserved to be loved by someone.

"Is it Faith?" he asked.

Parker gained control over her emotions. "I just went to check on her and she's struggling. They're hoping they won't have to move her."

"What can I do?" He sounded unsure and she remembered his words from yesterday, that he didn't plan to visit. He'd done his part by bringing her to the hospital.

That wasn't Matthew. Not the Matthew she knew. Not the Matthew whose sermons she'd listened to on podcasts.

"I—" She hesitated. She wouldn't say that she needed him. She couldn't give him that. It had been a mistake to call. A moment of weakness. "I just wanted you to know."

"I'll be praying," he assured her. It sounded as if he meant it. "Parker, I'm sorry."

"Me, too," she whispered. "I'll let you go. I'm going to hold her. Maybe it will help."

Help who? Her? Faith?

She returned to the nursery. The room was a good deal warmer than it had been when she left just minutes ago. Hazel smiled a greeting as she prepared their patient.

"You can pull the rocking chair over here," Hazel suggested, nodding her head in the direction of the chair. "I've got her all wrapped up and warm. Her little eyes are so dark and serious. I think she knows she's about to be treated to some loving arms. Poor babe hasn't had that since you brought her in yesterday."

"She should have her mommy's arms around her."

Hazel shook her head. "For some reason, her mommy must have thought she couldn't keep her. Probably in this one's best interest the mom picked that truck."

"Hmm." Parker made the sound in agreement with

the nurse, but her heart squeezed at the pronouncement. It seemed her heart hadn't stopped aching since she'd seen Matthew. All these years and she'd really thought herself over the pain his words had caused. She didn't want to imagine him being the best person for this baby to be left with. It didn't seem fair, in a way.

After speaking to the caseworker, she didn't want to imagine the future for a child left behind like trash on the side of the road.

She settled herself in the padded seat of the rocking chair and Hazel placed Faith in her arms.

"There you go, Parker. Hold her close and whisper some prayers for her."

Parker nodded and hugged Faith, giving her all the love she could in the short amount of time she had to give it.

As she held the baby, she prayed for her. She prayed for the right family—a mom and a dad—to love the little girl, care for her, raise her. She prayed for Faith's parents, whoever they might be. She prayed for herself, for wisdom. And then she sang to her and loved her.

The door to the nursery opened. Her heart skipped a beat, maybe three, as he entered the room. Tall, strong and very unsure. His dark eyes sought hers and then his gaze dropped to the bundle in her arms. He took off his black cowboy hat and with his free hand, took a swipe at his hair.

"You're here," she said.

"I know." He shrugged. "I didn't want to be involved, but I guess I am."

"Sometimes we don't have a choice."

He picked up a chair and brought it close, so close.

He leaned to watch as Faith slept in her arms. For

a long time, the two of them sat in silence, both focused on the infant, on her breaths and occasionally on the monitor attached to the wall. Her breathing, her heart and her oxygen all remained stable, even when she twitched and moved about.

"She's much prettier today than she was yesterday," he said after a while. "I've always felt guilty, lying to parents and telling them their newborns are the cutest thing ever. They're usually pretty wrinkled, red-faced and their heads are funny-shaped."

She laughed a little at the remark and Faith's eyes opened, to seek them with the tiniest turn of her head. She had dark hair and dark eyes and her cheeks were the faintest pink.

"She is beautiful," Parker said. "She'll get even prettier as she fills out."

"What will they do with her?" he asked as he put his finger in her tiny hand and watched those little fingers curl around his.

His question hurt, not that he intended that. It's just, she didn't want to think about Faith leaving, going to strangers. She didn't want to think about the short amount of time they, no *she*, would have with this baby girl.

At least she would have this time. Maybe that was God's plan—that she be here in this community hospital and even in Sunset Ridge, so that this baby would have a beginning with someone who cared for her.

The other thought, one that had been chasing through her mind and had kept her awake last night was that maybe, just maybe, God had brought the two of them, Matthew and herself, back to Sunset Ridge so she could see him face-to-face, forgive him and say good-bye. This would be the closure she hadn't realized she needed.

"Parker, are you okay?" Matthew's arm slipped around her back and he pulled her close, just briefly, offering comfort.

"Of course I am. I'm sure that once she's released, she'll go to foster care. Even if they find her mom, odds are the mom isn't clean and wouldn't be able to take custody."

"What a rotten way to start life. Why…?" He shook his head, not finishing the sentence.

She thought he probably meant to question where God had been when something like this happened. She remembered questioning God, more than once. It never meant she stopped believing. It just meant that sometimes it was difficult to understand the harder things in life—the things that hurt.

There were lessons in the hard times. If life could always be perfect, there would be no place for faith or even for growing and becoming a stronger person. That's how she preferred to think, to believe.

"What are you thinking?" he asked.

She reflected on the question. "You used to ask me that often when we were kids."

"Were we ever kids, Parker? I feel as if I've always been an adult."

"We were kids," she answered. "We skipped school a time or two, rode horses to the lake. Have you forgotten?"

He looked surprised by the mention of those carefree days.

"I haven't forgotten. I just haven't thought about it in a long time. I remember lying in the bed of the truck at the rodeo, staring up at the stars. Those were good times."

She closed her eyes at the words. It had been a fun, innocent moment. He hadn't touched her. They hadn't even held hands. After all, she'd been his best friend. The chunky girl with the pretty smile. Someone had actually written that in her senior yearbook.

"Yes, that was a good night. You won for team roping. You and Luke."

"You didn't answer my question," he reminded her. "What were you thinking about? Now."

"Storms. Life is full of storms. If life was always sunshine and roses, we would stop appreciating those beautiful days, the moments that make us sing with joy. We would fall apart the moment something difficult came our way because we wouldn't have the strength to persevere."

There, she'd said it. She watched as he digested her words, dissecting and taking them apart.

"That's all true, but some storms devastate."

"Yes," she agreed. "They do. And people rebuild. Often right where the storm did the most destruction."

She didn't tell him he would survive his storm. It wasn't her place to give him that reassurance and she knew he didn't want to hear it.

There was a purpose for everything under the sun. Even if it might hurt later, she knew that the weeks here would be a healing time for her. She would move on by putting the past to rest. This time, when she said goodbye to Sunset Ridge and to Matthew Rivers, it would be her choice, and she would be in control of her emotions and her future.

Chapter Four

A week after finding Faith, Matthew woke with a sudden start. He listened, thinking he'd heard something. The only noise was the dog snoring. Pete insisted they were best friends and he'd earned a right to sleep at the foot of the bed. All Pete's idea, not Matthew's.

Faith. The word, the name, wouldn't leave his mind. It was stuck there and refused to be shaken loose. He could sleep another hour or he could get up and make coffee. He could get out of bed and pray for the tiny baby girl.

He rolled out of bed, groaning at the time on his phone. Five o'clock.

"It's early," he said as he looked up. As if God was looking down, smiling at his unruly attitude. "My alarm goes off at six."

Silence.

"Thanks," he mumbled as he went to his knees in the small space at the side of the bed. Campers weren't meant for this. "I'm doing this for her. She deserves to live. She deserves to find parents who will cherish her and protect her. She deserves better than to start life abandoned and sick."

The words poured out, half-angry. No, full on angry. Angry that God hadn't answered his continuous prayers for his friend. He was angry for Jared's wife and children, left devastated by the loss of husband and father.

Angry that someone could dump a baby like she was nothing but trash to be tossed on the side of the road.

"This baby needs more days. She needs a strong heart and strong lungs. She needs love. Maybe she's meant to be Parker's baby. And maybe you can help Parker forgive me. Help me to be a better friend than the one who left here."

He pushed to his feet, afraid to acknowledge those prayers and the hope he had that God would listen.

"I'm still angry, but I can put aside my anger for that baby." He said the last as an addendum to his prayer as he stood there in the tiny bedroom of the camper he'd bought to serve as his home while he figured out his life.

He walked down the two steps to the kitchen-slash-living area, made himself a quick cup of coffee, pulled on his boots and headed for the barn. As he walked, the sun peeked over the eastern horizon and turned the morning from dark to light, just light enough to see the barn, the old farmhouse and the green fields that held more promise than they had in years. Decades.

He stopped for a minute, breathing in the fresh, spring air. It was the first of May and the cool mornings would soon be a thing of the past. He wanted to enjoy, just for a minute. Pete had followed him from the camper, but he trotted on to the barn. Matthew didn't hurry.

Cattle grazed and in the distance a rooster crowed.

For ten years he'd been telling himself he loved the big city, the noises, the smells, the constant activity. He'd told himself a few lies, one being that he didn't miss the country.

That didn't mean he planned on staying. He was just here to get his dad back on track and figure out where he would go next.

He was surprised to see lights on in the barn. As he entered, he saw his dad coming out of a stall. Buck looked as if he'd slept in that stall. Matthew remembered back to his childhood and Buck passing out after a night on the town. He always made it from his truck to the barn. They'd find him there the next morning.

"Where have you been?" Matthew asked, not a lick of sympathy or understanding in his tone. He didn't plan on being sympathetic.

As he stared his father down, he took a sip of scalding coffee.

"Right here in this barn since midnight last night," Buck shot back with a ferocious growl to the words.

Pete approached the two, giving them a low warning bark. Matthew ignored the dog.

"Are you keeping a bottle out here?" Matthew held his father's gaze, not bothering to hide the accusatory tone.

"Is that what you think?" Buck shook his head. "I should lay you out on your backside for that."

"Go for it. It wouldn't be the first time."

Now they were face-to-face, father and son. Years of anger and resentment brewed between the two of them. Matthew had forgiven him for all of it. At least, that's what he'd been telling himself since college, since the theology class that led him to believe he'd been called to ministry.

Or maybe he'd just felt that ministry might be a good fit for his skills. He'd learned that he could write and speak in a way that held everyone's attention. He was decent with people. He was a good person.

Buck jerked the hat off his head and squared up. "Let me tell you something, Mr. High and Mighty. I'm not drinking. And it isn't because you showed up. It's because I decided to quit. I decided to make my life right and let God change my heart. You're the one who's struggling and angry, not me. You can stay here until you're ready to move on, but you won't talk to me that way."

"Fine, I won't talk to you that way." Matthew stepped a little closer to his father, expecting bloodshot eyes and whiskey breath. There were neither.

"If you need to know, I was delivering a foal. I told you that mare you bought was close to delivering. She struggled all night and about thirty minutes ago, I had to help her out." Buck pointed at the stall. "If you'd taken a half second to look, you would have seen them in there."

Matthew walked to the stall and leaned to watch mare and foal as the baby got close and began to nurse. A shaft of early morning sunlight seeped into the room, just a beam sent to dance across the glistening gold of the mare and her matching foal. He'd wanted this mare for her color. Now there were two. The prettiest palomino mare he'd ever seen and her replica that pushed in close to nurse.

"Why didn't you come get me? I could have helped."

Buck shrugged off the too-late offer. "I handled it, kept her good and clean and made sure neither of them had any problems. Been a while since we had a foal on the place."

"Yeah, it has." Matthew glanced from the mare with her foal to his dad. "I'm sorry."

"Yeah, well, you're forgiven. I guess trust takes time. Now I'm going to the house to get some shut-eye and you can grain the cattle." Buck walked out the barn door, leaving Matthew alone with the mare, her foal and his thoughts.

He stood there with only the thoughts for company as he drank his coffee and watched the mare with her new baby. Pete wandered off, bored and probably hungry.

His phone rang. He glanced at the caller ID and sighed. The mare looked up, her ears pricking forward, as if questioning what might be the matter with him.

His brother Mark calling him at six in the morning couldn't be a good sign. He answered.

"Hey, big brother." Mark slurred the words in a happy voice.

"Give me a break. Are you seriously this person?" Matthew asked.

"Sorry, Preacher Boy, it is indeed who I am."

"Maybe you should stop and think who you're becoming," Matthew shot back. "Remember what we went through as kids?"

"Right," Mark said, his tone a little more serious. "Have you seen my wife and daughter?"

"I have, just not up close. I doubt she wants to talk to any of us." Matthew's brother Mark had managed to mess up his marriage, which led to his wife taking their daughter and moving out. One more act in the Rivers Family Drama, and Matthew was having enough trouble handling the one with his father.

"Probably not," Mark muttered. "She hasn't talked to me in a while."

"Can't say I blame her."

"I'm the reason she has the money for a bakery."

"You're the reason she's back home in Sunset Ridge, raising a daughter on her own. Your daughter," Matthew reminded him. "What do you want, Mark?"

"Just to talk to my big brother. At least you're always honest with me. Are you going to stay there and be a cattle rancher?"

"I'm not planning to stay. I'm just trying to get Dad back on his feet. He isn't healthy, you know."

"Yeah, you told me." Mark mumbled something. Matthew didn't ask him to repeat it. He probably didn't want to know what his brother said.

"How's that baby you found?" Mark asked after several long seconds of silence. Someone must have filled him in, Matthew thought. Small towns didn't need newspapers to spread the latest.

"She's good. I'm going to check on her after I take care of a few things around here." He hadn't planned on visiting again. He had a list of reasons why. He didn't want to get attached. She wasn't really his problem. There were people taking care of her.

This morning's prayer time had helped him realize, though, that he couldn't walk away.

"Did you get the money I sent?" Mark asked, his speech a little clearer.

"Yeah, thanks."

Matthew watched as the foal explored the stall. The little filly was all legs and fuzzy golden coat. "How's the music world?"

"Dog-eat-dog," Mark said. "I guess I need to get some sleep."

"By that you mean sleep it off?"

Mark laughed. "There's no fooling you, is there?"

"No, there isn't. Mark, get sober and be the man you wanted to be. I'm just guessing, but I'm sure your daughter needs you and wants you in her life."

"Right, I'll work on that." Mark hesitated. "Hey, don't break Parker's heart again. Talk to you later, Preacher."

Matthew looked at the now silent phone, considered calling his brother back and then rethought that decision. He slid the phone into his pocket and reached for his thermal coffee cup. If he meant to lecture his brother about his life choices, he guessed he'd have to take a few shots at his own past actions.

He left the barn, whistling for Pete as he headed for the truck. Cattle needed to be fed and fences still needed work. There was a lot to do on a place that had suffered decades of neglect. Neglect that he knew he couldn't fix overnight.

He tried to focus on what needed to be done, but Mark's warning about Parker couldn't be shaken off. Mark had befriended her after Matthew went to college. Mark had spent that last year with her, probably helping her through the broken heart caused by Matthew's abandonment and his parting words.

He hadn't known how to handle her declaration of love. He'd been too tied up in his own life and he hadn't thought about her feelings. After all, she'd been his best friend. She'd been the person who showed up his freshman year, pretty and funny, always joking. He'd needed someone like Parker—uncomplicated and easy to be around.

They'd gone to homecoming dances and proms together, because he didn't want to date and she never had a date. She'd joked that she would always be the best friend and never the girlfriend. He'd told her they were the perfect couple because he couldn't imagine himself as a husband, ever. She didn't want to date unless she planned on marrying the guy.

As he drove through the fields, Pete at his side, he realized how clueless his teen self had been. This reunion would be his opportunity to make things up to her. Rather than avoiding her, he'd spend time with her and they'd find a way to put the past behind them.

Unless she wanted nothing to do with him.

Parker sat down with her chicken salad sandwich, fresh from the cafeteria deli. She'd just come from visiting Faith. After a week, the infant seemed to be improving. She'd been weaned from oxygen and the infection was gone. She'd be going home soon. Or to a home. Whatever home the state picked for her since there was still no sign of her parents and they had no idea who her biological family might be.

A woman stepped through the doors of the cafeteria. She spotted Parker, waved and headed in Parker's direction. It didn't take Parker by surprise that the caseworker was visiting their young patient. She'd been to the hospital several times in the past week.

"Parker, they said I'd find you here. I hate to interrupt your lunch, but I wondered if we could talk."

Parker nodded to the empty chair across from her.

Jackie slid into the seat. "Thank you. I just checked on Faith. It appears she's doing really well."

"She's growing and getting stronger and healthier every day. No news on the mother?"

Jackie shook her head. "None. Even if we find Mom, odds are she's in no condition to raise this little girl."

"Have you found a family that can take her?"

Jackie shrugged. "The one home I had in mind is at a crossroads, wanting to have a child of their own. They're not sure if they can do this, not at the present time, but they're considering it."

"I can understand that."

They sat for several minutes. Parker nibbled a few bites of her sandwich, but the visit caused her to lose her appetite.

"I know we've had this conversation, but have you prayed about being a temporary placement?" Jackie finally asked. "We could do a kinship license, because you're really the only family she has."

"I have and I'll admit, I'm torn. I really do want to be the person who takes care of Faith. It's just so complicated."

"I know there are a lot of variables," Jackie said. "But for now, you're the only person spending real quality time with her. You visit her. You hold her. If she's bonded with anyone, it's you. Plus, you could put her in the hospital day care where you can be near her, even when you're working."

"I think the day care is at capacity," Parker said.

"It isn't," she said with a sly grin. "I checked. They have an opening. And they take infants."

Parker, queen of staying free from attachments, couldn't lie to herself or the caseworker. She was attached to Faith.

"I pray for her," Parker admitted. "I pray for her

health, for her mother and for the family that might take her. I've prayed that I could be the person."

Jackie's expression softened from caseworker to simply being a woman who cared and who was concerned for the baby in question. "I know, and I'm doing the same. I'm praying for both of you. There are no easy answers in this situation."

Parker remained silent, thinking over all of the reasons this would be a terrible idea.

A hand touched hers. Jackie gave her an understanding look. "I know you're filled with doubts. I'm not. I think you're the perfect mom for her. Faith is going to require that we all do some difficult and uncomfortable things on her behalf. As much as you are worried how your heart will feel when you part from her, imagine her little life, her heart and not having someone to love her and pray for her. Even a temporary relationship can make a difference in the life of a child."

"You're determined to make me cry," Parker said. She reached for a napkin to stem the tears that leaked out.

"I'm determined to put this baby in the best possible arms. I believe with all of my heart that those arms are yours." Jackie picked up her purse. "What about her rescuer, Mr. Rivers?"

"I haven't seen him in a few days," Parker said, not wanting to discuss Matthew.

"Hmm," Jackie responded. "Well, I'll leave you to your lunch, but I'll be in touch and you have my card."

Of course she would be in touch. And she would again ask if Parker might consider being a foster parent to baby Faith. Parker guessed that each time the caseworker asked the question, her defenses would be chipped away and it would get a little harder to say no.

Appetite lost, she took a few obligatory bites of her sandwich before dumping her tray and heading back to the ER. She almost walked past the door to the nursery, hesitated and then pushed the button to gain access to the hall.

Faith slept, her little thumb in her mouth—a sign she was ready for her next bottle. Parker knew the baby, knew her habits, her cries, her little grimaces. She loved the tiny little girl and no amount of staying away would undo those feelings.

"Hey, rosebud, you look pretty this morning. I've been praying for you." She glanced in the direction of the nurse, who was busy with a newborn. The nurse nodded permission and Parker lifted the baby girl from her bed.

Parker cuddled Faith close, singing to her as the infant nestled into her shoulder. The infant nuzzled in close. "Oh, Faith, I don't know what to do."

"She's grown."

His voice, coming from behind her, startled Parker. She jumped a little and then spun on her heel to face him. He was a good six inches taller than her five feet, six inches. Today he held a stuffed animal. Her heart gave a hefty thump at the sight of him with that plush, soft elephant in his hands. He was adorable when he was unsure. When his mouth hitched up on one side in that self-deprecating smile, her knees still went a little wobbly.

He held out the stuffed animal, forcing her attention to it and away from his face.

"They say it can be heated up in the microwave," he

explained. "I thought it might be nice for her, since she's alone in here, to have something warm to cuddle with."

"I'll ask the nurse if she can have it," Parker told him as she took the elephant and placed it in the basket on the side of the bed. "I didn't expect to see you."

He shrugged it off. "I tried to stay away. I obviously failed at that goal."

"It isn't so bad caring for her."

"No, it isn't. I just…" He shook his head and his gaze landed on the baby in her arms. "I don't know how to fix this for her. Or for you."

When he'd paused, she'd held her breath, wanting him to finish what he meant to say. Now that he had, she wasn't sure she liked his frank admission. For a moment he became her friend again, the one she'd lost all those years ago. He looked like that boy, unsure but willing to go to bat for her, to stand up for her.

The Matthew she'd known might deny it, but he cared deeply for the people in his life.

"The caseworker came by," Parker told him, needing someone else's opinion and needing neutral footing. "She asked me to be Faith's foster parent."

"I can see why," he said, watching as she held Faith close, kissing the top of her downy soft head. "It's obvious you love her."

"She's easy to love."

"Will you do it?" he asked as he put his pinky finger out for Faith to grasp.

"Is that what's best for her? Or am I just the convenient answer to the problem? She needs stability and I'm not that person. I'll be moving and I'm not sure where I'll go next."

"You could stay," he suggested, looking up, his eyes

grabbing and holding hers. He stood close to her side, close enough that she smelled soap, the mint of his toothpaste, noticed the dampness of freshly showered hair. She swallowed a dozen different emotions, the strongest being the instinct to flee.

"I don't think I can," she finally said.

He was quiet and she didn't elaborate.

"Look, I have to get back to work," she told him as she edged away, preparing to put Faith back in her warm bed.

"Do you think I could hold her?" he asked, not looking up from the baby's face. The softness of his voice, the uncertainty, was disarming.

"Of course." She spoke quickly, needing distance. "Do you want the rocking chair?"

In response, he pulled the chair close and settled in, his arms open for the baby she placed in them. He held Faith close, looking surprised and frightened all at the same time. He spoke to her in a quiet, reassuring voice, telling her everything would work out and she was going to be fine.

"I have to get back to work," Parker said again.

"I'll catch up with you later." He raised his head, seeking her eyes with his.

"Sure, of course." She hesitated at the door, watching the two of them together, envisioning a different path than the one she'd taken, a path that included a baby and a husband.

That path would never be hers and she felt its loss in a way she'd never felt before.

Chapter Five

Matthew saw the way Parker hesitated at the door. Her expression turned somber as she watched him with the baby. Longing, he thought might have been the look. She wanted Faith in her arms. She wanted to be the mother the little girl needed. He wanted that for her.

He didn't want Parker to wear that look of sadness, of having missed out. In all his thirty-six years on planet earth, he'd never needed so much to help another person find their happiness. Because she'd been his friend.

Maybe she could be his friend again? This time he would do better, treat her better.

Even if friendship didn't happen, he prayed for her because he knew the coming weeks wouldn't be easy and she'd be forced to make a life-altering decision.

"Here I am, praying again," he mumbled to the ceiling. "I'm not even sure what to do about my own life, my future, and I can't stop long enough to figure it out."

In his arms, Faith wiggled and drew his attention back to her, to her life and situation. "You're about the prettiest thing I've ever seen."

Parker's face flashed to mind. "Let me tell you about

the woman who is fighting herself, wanting to be your mom and not wanting to get attached. She's special. She knows how to find joy in the worst situations. She tells the corniest jokes. She has the prettiest smile and the truest brown eyes I've ever known. I missed her and now, I'm glad she's here, because I think you need her."

The infant in his arms looked up, her dark eyes alert and studying his face. He felt a little bit of his heart thaw and it ached, the way fingers ache when a person comes in from the cold and runs them under warm water.

Poetic thoughts. He shook his head.

"See what you do to me, little girl? You have me thinking like a poet. I'm definitely not a poet. What do you think of Parker?"

She opened her tiny mouth and cooed. It was the first time he'd heard a noise from her other than the pitiful cries of that first day. The noise captured him and he couldn't have been more enthralled. He'd been to Hawaii, to the Grand Canyon and to Paris. Seeing those places had never moved him the way that little sound did.

He closed his eyes, sighing. That tiny coo and the look on Parker's face when she'd held the baby close, singing to her. Both were wrapped up in one package and probably the eighth wonder of the world.

Faith slept in his arms, snuggled close to his chest—to his heart. He thought about her future and her mother, who was out there somewhere. He guessed that the mother might be just a kid. Maybe a kid in need of help. That broke him a little.

He started to pray but his thoughts shattered. Did God listen to a man who doubted his own faith, his own sincerity? He was pretty sure his prayers wouldn't qualify as the "effectual fervent prayers of a righteous man."

A monitor beeped. He glanced down at the bundle in his arms, wondering what it meant. The nurse rushed to his side and, without words, took Faith.

"Hey, little one, what's up with this?" The nurse placed her back in the warming bed and put a stethoscope to her heart.

"What's going on?" He leaned close on the other side, watching Faith, watching monitors.

He studied the numbers and then saw that it was the pulse ox that had dropped. It lowered to 80 percent as the monitor continued to beep. Another nurse joined the first. They moved quickly, attaching a nasal cannula. They continued to monitor their patient as he stood back.

He bowed his head and said a quick prayer that felt more like pleading for God to listen. *Just do this one thing. Not for me, but for Faith. For Parker. Please.*

Her oxygen levels slowly climbed back to normal. Her coloring pinked up again. The nurses discussed the hope that she wouldn't need to be placed back on a respirator. The second nurse left to call the doctor.

"You're going to have to go now," Nurse—he looked at her nametag—Aubree, told him. "We need to let her rest."

"Will you call if there are any changes?" he asked.

"You know we can't do that. There are laws, and you're not family or a guardian. You understand that you're given special privileges because you found her and this is a small hospital?"

"I get that. Let Parker know?"

She nodded and went back to work. He left the nursery with one backward glance to make sure all was well and the monitor continued to show steady, healthy numbers.

The last thing he wanted to do was leave the hospital. He knew the staff would do a great job tending to her. They cared about her. Like it or not, she'd become a part of his life that day he found her and leaving felt like abandoning.

He walked down the hall, not sure where he would go or what he would do; he just knew he couldn't leave.

As he made his way through the small community hospital, he could hear the hushed whispers of nurses at their station and the occasional conversation from a hospital room. He realized his steps were taking him in the direction of the small chapel. He could sit there and think, maybe pray.

"Hello out there. Who is that?" The voice, a woman's, came from one of the rooms.

Matthew kept walking.

"You come back here right now."

He hesitated and then spun on his heel to return to the room. Late afternoon sunlight seeped through the drawn curtains, giving faint light, but enough to see the woman sitting up in her bed. She raised her chin and then beckoned him inside.

"I know you," she said.

"Do you?" He gave her a curious look. She didn't seem familiar.

"Matthew Rivers from Sunset Ridge. I was your fifth grade teacher."

"Miss Philips." He did know her. Taking a closer look, he realized she still had the same distinctive cheekbones, the same scolding blue eyes. Now he could see laughter in those eyes. As a boy, she'd frightened the life out of him.

"Sit down. You're not in trouble."

"You've said that before." He gave her a speculative look.

"Well, this time I mean it. I thought I saw you traipsing the halls. Why are you here?"

"I'm visiting a baby in the nursery."

"The one found in the back of a truck. Was that your truck? I thought you were a big city preacher in Chicago. Now, I can admit, I never saw that one coming."

"Oh?" He didn't know if he should laugh or be offended. He laughed. "I didn't see it coming, either."

"Mind you, you weren't one that I thought would end up in jail. Your brother Mark and that Jonah, both seemed to be headed for trouble."

"They're both doing well. Mark is in Nashville and Jonah rides bulls and lives in Texas." Maybe *doing well* was an exaggeration.

"I've heard Mark on the radio. I've also read some stories that aren't too flattering," she admitted. "But you, you're back in Sunset?"

"I am." Reunion over. He started to move from the chair. She stayed him with a hand and a look.

"Don't go just yet." Her voice became soft, nearly quivering.

"I should let you rest."

"I've been resting for two days and I want to go home. Unfortunately, I've got an infection and can't leave just yet," she informed him in her prim schoolteacher voice. "I don't know if you're aware, but I never married and I never had children. I didn't picture myself in a hospital bed with no one to visit."

"I'm sorry," he told her as he settled back in the chair, knowing he'd be there for a bit. He meant it, that he was sorry, but the words never seemed to convey the real feeling behind them.

"I can see that you're sincere," she said as she settled back against her pillows. "It does get lonely. I have an occasional visitor from town, but they don't stay long."

"That must be hard. When do you think they'll let you go home?"

"It could be days, or a week. Or…" She shook her head. "Well. I'm not going to get melancholy."

He understood her meaning and his heart sank a little. He didn't really know Miss Philips, but in this moment, he realized he was her friend. Her neighbor. She was frail, alone and trying to be strong.

"Would you stay for a while?" she asked. "The company would be nice and you have a good voice. I'd like for you to read to me. They loaded me in that ambulance without my glasses."

He must have looked unsure because she continued. "That's a lot to ask of a former student, isn't it?"

And yet, she handed him the Bible from the table next to her bed.

"It isn't too much to ask." He'd done this before for members of his church. It wouldn't hurt him to spend some time with this lady who had given so much to teach children in their community. "When I leave, is there anything I can do for you at your house?"

"Well, since you asked, feed my cat and bring me my glasses," she said in a cheerful voice, her blue eyes sparkling. "Now read for me, Matthew Rivers. I like to know that I did something for you Rivers boys. If you can read and know a bit about history and math, I accomplished something."

"I can read," he told her as he opened the Bible and found where she'd marked Psalm 91. He began to read. "He that dwelleth in the secret place of the most High shall abide under the shadow of the Almighty."

He let his voice rise and fall as she settled back in her bed, a contented expression on her face.

This place felt too familiar to Matthew. He'd been here dozens of times before, with a patient needing solace, needing prayer, needing a friend. Pastor Matthew Rivers had been there for his parishioners. He'd been there for his friend Jared, as much as he'd been allowed, that is. To the very end. To the very last prayer—the one that had begged God to be merciful and spare his friend, raise him up from the sickbed, give him back to his family.

He choked on the words of Psalm 91 as emotion rolled through him.

Miss Philips's eyes opened. She hadn't been sleeping as he'd assumed. "Matthew, are you well?"

"Sorry." He squeezed the bridge of his nose between his thumb and finger. "I'm good."

"Is that so?" she asked.

He felt a flicker of humor. "I'm doing my best."

"I guess coming home is easier if you're running from something that is worse than what you're coming home to." She arched a brow as she said the tangle of words. "Have you talked to anyone about this?"

"I haven't," he admitted, surprised at how easily he could answer her.

"If you can't tell anyone else, you can always talk to

God. He's been my closest companion for seventy-nine years and He's never once been 'too busy to listen.'"

"But does He always answer?" The words slipped through his defenses.

"He never fails to answer, but the answer isn't always the one we think we want."

"Have you ever prayed for a miracle and…?"

She pushed the button on her bed to raise herself up. "I've prayed for so many. I prayed for a husband, but a husband never came. I prayed hard for that husband. I wanted a family. Eventually I accepted that my life was exactly what it was meant to be and when I accepted, I found peace and I found joy. I became content. Contentment is a gift."

"Hmm." His response was noncommittal.

"Some people make 'content' seem like a bad thing. As if being content with our lives means we aren't seeking more. To me, 'content' means that I've found a way to accept my situation and there is joy in that acceptance."

"I think I probably learned a lot in fifth grade." Matthew smiled as he said this. "But I think I learned a lot more in this conversation."

"Life lessons are sometimes the hardest. Give it time and you'll find healing, and contentment."

"Thank you, Miss Philips."

"You're very welcome, Pastor Matthew."

"I'm no longer a pastor. I've taken a leave of absence." He closed her Bible, leaving the bookmark at Psalm 91. *He that dwelleth in the secret place of the most High…*

"Oh, I see, God recalled the calling? As if you're a car with a defective engine?" Her soft cheeks folded into a dimpled grin. "Don't look at me like that. I'm seventy-nine and I can say things that other people can't."

He chuckled at the comment. "You're right, and since you're so honest, I'll be honest. I don't know that I was ever called to ministry. I took a class in theology and I realized I enjoyed speaking. I enjoyed writing sermons. It felt natural. I'm not sure if that equals being called or if I just saw it as a good career option."

"I applaud your honesty. You were always a good student and I can see how you found this to be your niche. I'll be praying for you, Matthew. I would ask a favor. Visit me from time to time and, when I'm gone, will you preach my funeral?"

"I don't see that happening anytime soon."

"But you'll do it?"

He only had to think about it for a moment.

"Yes, I'll do that for you. I'll also feed your cat."

She reached for his hand, taking it in a stronger grip than he would have imagined. "And now, if you'll pray for me before you go, I'd appreciate it."

He nodded, agreeing to this prayer because even if his faith wasn't sure, hers seemed to be strong enough for them both. Fighting emotion and memories, he cleared his throat and bowed his head.

He prayed for Miss Philips and he added baby Faith to the prayer. She gave his hand a gentle squeeze as he said "amen" and then her hand slid from his.

She wiped a tear from her cheek. "Go on now. And next time you visit, I want another prayer like that one. It touched my soul, Matthew Rivers. It brought to mind several prayers that I prayed for you over the years. Look at what God has done."

The comment meant something and he should have replied to it, but he couldn't. Instead, he remembered her request. "How do I feed the cat?"

"There's a key under the flowerpot. My cat's name is Sam and his food is in the kitchen. My reading glasses are on the counter." She gave him her address.

"I'll take care of both."

He touched her hand, frail but strong, and he left the room. As he entered the hall, he saw Parker standing a short distance away. Parker, with her blond streaked hair held back by a scarf that matched her pink scrubs. Parker, always smiling, always encouraging. She swiped at the tear that rolled down her cheek. He felt a little raw with emotion and seeing her there nearly undid him. He couldn't escape, possibly didn't want to, so he allowed himself to walk up to her, not sure what he was going to say.

"That was beautiful," she told him, reaching for his hand. The gesture seemed natural, but then it wasn't. She slid her hand from his and searched for conversation that would ease them apart. "Miss Philips attended our church when my dad preached in Sunset Ridge."

"She was my fifth grade teacher."

Now they were back on firm footing.

"I was going to see Faith again before I leave for the day. Do you want to walk with me?" she asked.

He glanced at his watch and she kind of hoped he would say he had somewhere to be. If he left, they could part with easy congeniality between them. Friends. Or onetime friends. Acquaintances who would briefly share another moment with an infant girl before going their separate ways again. She mulled it all through her mind, while secretly crossing her fingers and now hoping he would say yes.

He shrugged and said, "Sounds good to me."

Together they walked down the hall. When they reached the double doors that led to the nursery, Matthew hurried forward to press the button and then open the door for her. He'd always been that person. He was a door opening, women-first kind of cowboy. Even citified, he still wore that black cowboy hat and cowboy boots, though the boots he wore today weren't the rough, muddy ones of his youth.

He opened the second door. She entered the nursery ahead of him and stopped to wash her hands before heading for the incubator where Faith slept. Her tiny hand was fisted and curled up against her cheek. Her rosebud mouth quirked upward and her eyelids fluttered.

"She's having good dreams," Matthew said. "Or do babies dream? They would need memories to dream?"

"They don't dream at this age, but they do spend a lot of time in REM sleep patterns and their little brains are developing. I don't know that we would want her to dream of the traumatic things she has been through." Even if she didn't remember what had happened, trauma did affect tiny brains.

"She's been through a lot, but she's also been held by you." He said it so simply and sweetly. He said it as if being held by her mattered.

She swallowed past the tightness in her throat, telling herself his words meant nothing.

"We should go," Parker said, letting herself touch the baby's curled hand one last time. "I don't want to wake her. Sleep is important to these little ones."

"If the cafeteria is open, I could buy you a piece of

pie." Matthew made the offer as they were leaving the nursery.

She nearly accepted, but then thought better of it. "I can't. I'm dieting."

"Dieting? Why?" He looked truly surprised.

She shouldn't be shocked by that. He'd never noticed her weight. She always assumed that because they were friends it didn't matter to him. She wasn't that same chunky teen, but she still fought the battle, carrying extra weight when her friends found it so easy to maintain.

"I'm trying to stay healthy," she told him. She'd learned to make her eating choices about health and not weight loss.

He merely nodded, not arguing her out of the choice. "Coffee?"

"No, I think I'm ready to go home. I have to be back here at six in the morning."

"I'll walk you to your car."

"I'll take you up on that."

They headed outside where the weather was warm and sultry, the promise of summer in the air. After a long day inside, Parker had to stop and breathe in.

"This is so nice," she whispered, opening her eyes to see him smiling down at her.

"You always loved spring."

"I still do. It's the promise of new beginnings, I guess."

"Do you want to walk around the block? There's a garden and the flowers are blooming."

"Yes, that would be nice."

Yes, it would be very pleasant, but maybe not wise. Matthew still held a special place in her heart, and she didn't need to be reminded of that by being with him when it wasn't really necessary.

She couldn't always make the right choices. The temptation of a walk in the garden after a long day inside dealing with everything from cut fingers to heart attacks had taken a toll and she needed a moment to breathe and relax.

He took her hand as they crossed the street to the sidewalk that circled the hospital. The flower garden sat tucked away in a corner of the building. A fountain trickled and splashed. A hummingbird flitted through the air and hovered over one flower before moving to another.

"I'm not sure why I picked nursing. It keeps me inside and I love being outside. I could have been a gardener. Gardening would be far less stressful."

"You love helping people," he reminded.

"I do. It must be a by-product of being a pastor's daughter."

"I think it's just who you are."

"Do you? Because really, you don't know me that well." She faced him now and she immediately regretted those words and the way his eyes widened in surprise. "I shouldn't have said that."

"You have every right." He reached out and pushed a tendril of her hair behind her ear. His touch was barely-there soft, but she felt it to her toes. "Parker, I am sorry. The last thing I meant to do was hurt you. I was surprised that you felt that way about me. Shocked, really, because I didn't expect those words."

"I have a hard time believing you were that surprised," she said. "I felt I was pretty obvious."

"Maybe I chose not to see? I didn't want anything

to change a friendship that meant a lot to me. I'd like nothing more than for us to be friends again."

"I'm not sure if I can, Matthew." She wasn't clear on how to put the words in an order that made sense. It was embarrassing to return to those days, the phone call, all of it. "I made a huge mistake calling you. I guess I thought I had that one chance, so why not take it and tell you how I felt? And when you laughed..."

She'd been devastated. Heartbroken. She'd struggled with that rejection. It had nearly wrecked her. She had always felt confident. She'd managed to convince others that she was confident. And then he'd stripped away the mirage of self-assurance by laughing at her. That night she looked in the mirror and saw a stranger, an overweight teenager no one would ever love. She'd never seen that person before, never saw herself that way.

It had taken a long time for the wound to heal and for her to like the person in the mirror.

"I was a stupid kid," he said softly. "I didn't know what to do with those words. You were Parker, my best friend."

Yes, always the best friend. She had to walk away from him to keep from saying it out loud.

"Parker," he called out, no longer that stupid boy. He hurried after her. "I'm so sorry."

She stopped at a bench and sat down. "It was a long time ago and it's over. Water under the bridge."

He sat down next to her. "Is it really?"

"Yes. It took time, but it's over and done with." She wanted to believe that, but it was hard.

"So, we can be friends?"

"You're not giving up, are you?"

He laughed and the sound drew her. She leaned a

little in his direction as he leaned in hers. Their shoulders bumped. Against her will, her lips tugged upward, amusement finding her.

"I'm not giving up."

What would it hurt? she asked herself, knowing the answer. It would hurt her heart, because friendship for a season looked like this—temporary.

"I guess we can be friends for now, since we will be bumping into each other when we visit the nursery. You plan on visiting from time to time?"

"After holding her, I don't think I can stay away."

"I'm glad," she said, leaving it at that.

They sat in silence for a while, watching the sun drift down on the western horizon. Butterflies flitted around the flowers and in the distance, the sound of an ambulance cut the quiet.

"I should go," she said after a time.

"Same. I promised Miss Philips I'd take care of her cat."

"You're a softy. First babies, now cats. Oh, and Buck. What next?" she teased.

They were walking in the direction of her car.

"I'm afraid to think about it," he finally answered.

"Maybe you could be Faith's foster parent?"

His teeth flashed white in his tanned face and humor settled over his features. He looked down at her, reminding her of how it had felt to be his friend. She'd loved those years. And him. She didn't love him now. Obviously. Maybe she needed to keep telling herself that.

"As much as I appreciate your wisdom, I think that would be a bad idea. I've never changed a diaper and probably never will."

"Never say never," she found herself teasing. It felt

good to tease, to find a lighter mood. “You could take the job at the Sunset Ridge Community Church, help bring that dusty old ranch back to life and raise Faith. Buck would be Grampa Buck.”

“Too far!”

When they reached her car, he opened the door for her and then the two of them stood there in awkward silence. She should say good-bye, get in and drive away.

“I’ll see you later.” She still didn’t move.

“I’m sure we will be seeing a lot of each other,” he said. “Goodbye, Parker.”

And then he kissed her. It wasn’t a moonlight and romance kind of kiss, just a sweet, gentle kiss. And yet, as he pulled away, they both drew back, taking a breath and staring at each other.

“I shouldn’t have,” he said.

“Probably not.” She attempted to smile, to put him at ease. Should she tell him she was glad he had? No, she shouldn’t tell him and she shouldn’t be glad. She got in her car, pretending to be confident and not the least bit affected by a kiss.

She even managed to flip her hair over her shoulder and give him a cheeky smile. It all felt terribly false.

Parker Smythe had never been a hair toss kind of girl. Matthew Rivers had always been a broken heart waiting to happen. It would be best to avoid him as much as possible, because she clearly hadn’t gotten over him.

Chapter Six

The next morning, as Matthew headed for his truck, he spotted his dad hobbling toward the barn. Matthew watched the painful process of Buck's stride, the way he favored his right leg, but then realized the left hurt just as badly. He had to convince his father to go to the doctor. Even if Buck having knee surgery put Matthew here longer than the few months he'd expected to stay, it had to be done.

Buck spotted him and headed his way.

"Where are you off to?" Buck asked as he reached the truck, winded and holding his hand to his heart.

"You going to make it?" Matthew asked, more concerned than the words probably conveyed.

"Yeah, I'm gonna make it," Buck mimicked. "I'm old, but I don't have one foot in the grave."

"I know you don't." Matthew pulled his keys out of his pocket. "I've got a few errands to run."

Buck stood there, waiting.

"Do you want to go with me?" Matthew asked, because he knew that's what Buck was waiting for.

"Sure do." Buck hobbled around the truck to the passenger side.

Matthew got behind the wheel and waited for Buck to clamber in. He remembered his promise to Miss Philips. He had to go by her place and check on the cat named Sam and get her reading glasses.

"I need to run by Miss Philips's house."

His dad clicked his seatbelt in place before giving him a questioning look. Buck had shaved that morning. First time in a while. Maybe they were making progress. Maybe Buck really was on the wagon to stay.

"I heard she has heart failure," Buck said with genuine sympathy. "Took her out of her place in an ambulance."

"Yes, she's in the hospital. She asked me to feed her cat."

"And you agreed?" Buck shook his head and chuckled lightly. "You're a pushover."

"I'm trying to do something nice for a neighbor."

"She lives in town and has neighbors that actually live close by."

"I told her I'd do it," Matthew said as he shifted his truck into gear. Buck had a way of pushing him to the limit of his patience. Maybe he tried or maybe it was just a natural occurrence but, either way, Matthew didn't want to argue.

"Fine, do what you need to do."

He let his dad have the last word and started down the driveway. Maybe none of this was what he needed to do. Maybe it wasn't even what he wanted to do. He was just going along until he figured out what came next.

"What's wrong with you?" Buck asked as they eased

down the driveway, going as slow as possible to avoid the many ruts and potholes.

"The driveway is a mess," Matthew answered.

"I meant why do you have a death grip on the steering wheel?"

"No reason."

Matthew relaxed his hands. He didn't want to tell Buck that he didn't have a clue what he was going to do with his life. He woke up every day hoping the path would be clear. Instead, he found new obstacles, new obligations, new confusion each morning, and he no longer had the heart to pray for direction. He had the summer to figure it out and then he'd have to decide if he would resume his position as pastor or resign.

If he resigned, then what? He'd written a few books on faith, put some money aside and had no debt, so he guessed he had time to figure it out.

Silence held them for a long minute. They were on the paved road heading to town when Buck coughed a little. Matthew glanced his way for mere seconds before refocusing on the drive.

"I'm sorry," Buck said. "I know it must have been tough losing your friend."

"Yeah," Matthew said. He hoped they could leave it at that because he wasn't used to Buck being insightful.

"How about the preacher's daughter? I guess you didn't know she'd be back in town." Buck managed an amused look and a teasing tone. That had always been Buck's way of lightening the mood. If the conversation got too deep, Buck changed it.

"No, I didn't know she'd be here. Stop calling her that. Her name is Parker."

"I know it is, but it riles you when I call her the other."

"It doesn't *rile* me," Matthew denied. "I just think you should have respect."

"Fine, I won't call her anything other than Parker." Buck was silent for a moment or two. "I was told you made an offer on the Jackson place."

They were a half mile outside of Sunset Ridge. Matthew slowed his truck, giving them a little time to talk before reaching their destination.

"I did. I signed a contract."

"And then what?" His father asked.

Then what? Matthew hadn't really given that question much thought. He'd wanted the land and he'd made an offer. Then what? Would he live in the large, craftsman-style house with its wide front porches and kitchen windows that overlooked the creek? What would he do with the place, the house, the barns?

Make it a part of the family ranch and rent the house? Buy cattle and horses and call it his home? What would he do in Sunset Ridge? Take a job somewhere in Tulsa? Maybe he'd write another book, one about questioning his faith, but it probably wouldn't go over well with readers of his other works. They wouldn't want to hear that he'd lost faith, grown angry, jaded and maybe even disillusioned.

When he'd made the offer on the property, his only thought was it would help his dad and be a good investment, and he was looking for ways to build security without investing in risky stocks or similar products. He hadn't thought of sticking around, but after he'd inked his name, more and more, he felt happy about the idea that he now had a place to call his own, to go to when he was troubled.

"I guess you don't have to decide right away what

you plan to do," Buck said in another rare moment of insightfulness. "But thank you for buying it. I have a lot of regrets. My family falling apart and losing the land are at the top of the list."

"We all have regrets," Matthew knew that as well as anyone.

He turned down the side road that led to their destination.

Miss Philips lived on a dead-end street a few blocks off the square in Sunset Ridge. It was a tree-lined street with older homes and big lawns. Matthew turned into the driveway of the brick ranch-style home.

"Are you getting out?" he asked his father.

"Nah, I'll sit here and rest my knees." That was the closest Buck had come to actually admitting to his pain.

"I won't be long."

He easily found the key that Miss Philips had hidden—and guessed that if someone wanted to break in, they could also find it. He unlocked the door and entered the dimly lit home. The curtains were all closed tight and the air was on, but just enough to keep the heat at bay. There didn't seem to be a cat in sight. He went to the kitchen and rummaged around, and he found the cat food and then the feeder that held enough for several days.

He was leaning to pick up the feeder when he heard the wild beast. It half meowed and half growled just before it jumped off the fridge. He fended it off, not wanting to hurt it, but unwilling to let it scratch his face.

"Get off," Matthew ordered as he brushed the cat away and sidestepped the feline attacker. The cat snatched at his hand, its claws snagging the skin.

"You maniac." Matthew jerked his hand back at the

sting of pain. "Maybe I shouldn't have taken pity on you and come here to feed you."

"Hello? Anyone here?"

Matthew groaned inwardly at the familiar voice.

"I'm in the kitchen," he called out as he turned on the faucet and ran his hand under cold water. The cat, seemingly over his anger or whatever had possessed him to attack, rubbed against Matthew's legs, purring.

Parker entered the kitchen, a puzzled expression narrowing her eyes. She watched as he blotted the scratch with a paper towel and then grabbed more to stem the flow of blood. He glared at the cat who now sat next to him, licking its paws.

"Evil," he whispered at the animal.

"I didn't expect to see *you* here," he said to Parker. "Did Miss Philips send us both to feed her cat?"

"No, but I saw you pull in and thought I'd offer to help. Let me look at that."

He removed the paper towel. "It's fine. Just a scratch."

"A cat scratch can be a nasty thing if it gets infected," she warned.

Right, but he couldn't stand next to her and not think about the kiss. It had been a moment and he didn't regret the sweetness of it. He'd actually been thinking about that kiss and how he'd like to repeat it.

She reached for his hand and he gave it to her. She gave it a thorough look, then a cleaning that burned.

"Ouch," he said, trying to pull back.

"Don't be a baby," she said sweetly. "It needs to be clean, not just wiped."

"I think you're enjoying causing me pain."

She gave him a cheery look. "Maybe."

Sam hopped from the floor to the kitchen counter

to watch the process. “Now you want to be friends? Or are you also enjoying watching my pain?”

The cat stretched, kneading his front paws on the dish towel. His amber eyes seemed friendly enough and his orange coat was thick and shiny. He was a very loved cat. He probably missed his friend, and for that reason Matthew would give him a pass.

“He got you really good,” Parker said, her tone half serious and half amused. “I’m sure there are bandages around here somewhere and some antibiotic salve.”

“Thank you.” He reached for a paper towel and dried his hand by blotting. “I’m sure it’s fine. I’ve had worse.”

“I’m sure you have, but let me do this. There’s a lot of bacteria in those claws.”

She left but returned just minutes later with a first aid kit. “Let me see your hand.”

From the front of the house a door closed.

“You all in here?” Buck called out.

“In the kitchen,” Matthew answered with a sigh. The last thing he needed was Buck watching and finding this all too amusing.

Parker, leaning to get a good look at his hand as she applied the salve, happened to look up at that moment. Their gazes connected for a breath. She was so close, her honey-streaked hair hanging loose, a few strands in her face.

“Don’t look at me that way.” She said it on a breathless whisper. “Your dad will be here in ten seconds.”

Right, his dad.

“Sorry, I…” *I what?*

Fortunately, Buck entered the room and he couldn’t give the answer that had been on his mind. He wanted to kiss her again. Simple enough, but not simple at all.

He had to let it go. He'd always known that a relationship between them would be disastrous. She was too sweet and too good for someone like him. Having Buck in the room served as a reminder. Matthew didn't know the first thing about how to be a husband, or a father.

He'd known as a teenager, just the same way he knew now, that a relationship with Parker would end with her being hurt and that's why he'd never allowed them to be more than friends. She deserved the very best and Matthew would never be the very best.

Parker took a quick step away from Matthew and turned to face Buck Rivers as he entered the kitchen. He had a mischievous grin on his face and his gray eyes twinkled as he looked from one to the other of them.

Matthew resembled his father. She could see in Buck the man that Matthew would be in another thirty years. Except Matthew would never have the haggard appearance of someone who had lived a rough and somewhat devastating life. A difficult life. It showed in every line on his face and in the slight stoop with which he walked.

"I was getting worried," Buck said with a convincing look of concern.

"I told you it would be a minute," Matthew said as he patted the adhesive strip across the scratch.

Buck didn't miss a thing. "Cat attack?"

"Yeah, something like that."

"I've never had a use for them as anything other than barn animals. They do keep down the rodent population."

"Since you're feeding Sam, I guess I can go." Parker didn't care how desperate the escape appeared. It was past time for her to exit this situation.

"Wait, her reading glasses," Matthew said. "She asked me to get them, but she said they were on the counter. They aren't. Do you have any idea where they'd be?"

"My guess would be next to her chair where she sits to read her Bible." She felt a little sympathy for him as he avoided his new friend, Sam. "Want me to feed him tomorrow?"

"I don't mind feeding him." He moved his arm, to keep the cat from rubbing against him. Sam hopped from the counter to the floor and rubbed against his feet. "But we're not going to be friends."

"I think Sam's decided you *will* be friends." Parker smoothed her hand down the sleek fur of the cat.

They found Miss Philips's reading glasses and went out the front door together. Matthew locked the house up and placed the key in its hiding place.

"Where's your car?" he asked Parker as they went down the sidewalk.

"I'm not a creepy stalker who followed you here," she told him. "I live next door with Erma Adams. The hospital has a contract with her, renting one or two bedrooms for traveling medical staff."

"She retired from the hospital, didn't she?" Buck asked.

"Yes, she did."

"Parker, you ought to come have breakfast with us," Buck Rivers said, clearly out of the blue. And yet, with an expression that made her uneasy. She'd had enough of well-meaning matchmakers to last a lifetime. Everyone had a son, grandson, co-worker or neighbor that she should meet.

"I'd love to, but I need to catch up on laundry." She backed away.

"You can't do all that work without eating a good breakfast," Buck continued. "Isn't that right, son?"

At the affectionate term, son, Matthew jerked around, appearing to be at a loss. Parker understood, because she'd known better than most the type of abuse Matthew and the other boys had suffered. Buck could be funny and charming, but drunk, he became violent.

If she had to guess, he'd spent more time being violent than charming.

Matthew faced her and they shared a moment of understanding that Buck didn't notice before Matthew gave a quick nod.

"You should join us. We're actually going out to the Jackson place. I'm going to look at a few horses and some cattle that they're interested in selling."

"Well now, you didn't tell me that." Buck radiated happiness. "I'll give you the front, Parker."

"I'm not…"

She wasn't. She truly wasn't going.

Matthew interrupted her objections. "You should join us. It's Tuesday and Chuck makes his special French toast on Tuesday. Homemade bread and his secret egg dip."

"Secret egg dip?" Now she was curious.

"What you dip the bread in. It's a secret that Chuck won't share, but it's mighty fine French toast." This from Buck.

She hadn't expected Matthew's father to be a French toast connoisseur. The fact brought a smile that she also didn't expect. She wondered if Matthew was sorry he'd bumped into her. First a cat scratch and now his father inviting her to join them for breakfast.

"We can bring you back after breakfast." The offer seemed genuine and it broke down all of her doubts, her hesitation.

They used to meet once or twice a week for a meal at Chuck's.

"I'll go." She said it, knowing she might regret it later. "Let me grab my purse."

"I'll pull over to Mrs. Adams's driveway." He was already walking back to his truck. He was tall, confident, a lot of cowboy and a touch of city.

Thirteen. That's how old she'd been when they'd met. What a tough time in a girl's life. Everything changed at thirteen. Acne developed, crushes seemed life-altering, moving and leaving friends seemed like the end of the world. God had seen fit to take them from Oklahoma City to the small town of Sunset Ridge where being new meant being seen. She'd been a chubby kid with nondescript brown hair and brown eyes.

Matthew had instantly taken her into his group. The acceptance had changed her life.

A few minutes later she was in his truck. His dad had moved to the back, leaving the front passenger seat for her.

Matthew shot her a look and she saw the twinkle of amusement in his gray eyes. He must also be thinking that his father had pulled a fast one. She also noticed, but only because she had a nose, that he smelled like a forest, but also like spices and sunshine. Anyone who had a nose would have noticed the same.

They arrived at Chuck's five minutes later. Matthew pulled into the same spot where he'd parked the last time they'd seen each other here. The day he'd found Faith. As they got out, she noticed he did a quick surveillance of the area. As if he expected to see that rusted out sedan leaving the scene of the crime.

Together the three of them crossed the street to Chuck's. On the next block of the square was Kylie's Coffee Shop and Bakery—the place Parker had gone to several times since coming to town. Kylie Rivers. Matthew's ex-sister-in-law and the mother of his niece. What a broken family.

Matthew noticed the direction in which she'd looked.

"I saw her the other day," he said it quietly. "And Junie. She's an amazing little girl."

Buck had walked on ahead of them and was already going through the door to Chuck's.

"She's very smart," Parker agreed. "And adorable."

"Too bad my brother can't get his act together."

"Unfortunately, it isn't always as easy as wishing. Kylie knows that, but can't spend her life waiting for him to be a better man."

"I hurt for them," Matthew admitted.

She knew that he did. She also wondered if he ever thought about what a decent and good man he was, or did he put himself in the same category as his brother?

The idea that he wouldn't allow himself to have a family because he might hurt them—the way his dad had hurt his family, or the way Mark had hurt his—broke her heart. Matthew Rivers was a man worth loving and a man who deserved to be loved.

Chapter Seven

They entered the busy diner, Matthew holding the door for Parker. Heads swiveled to see who the newcomers were and a few eyes widened. Whispered comments flew between the customers. Matthew fought the urge to back out of the door slowly and run for his life.

"Too late to leave," Parker said. At least she could find amusement in the situation.

Or was it amusement? He took a deeper look into eyes the color of dark honey and he wondered if his hesitancy had hurt her feelings. He didn't want to hurt her, he never had wanted that.

"I'm not leaving," he assured her. He grinned, hoping to ease the tension. "We're in this together."

His dad beckoned from his regular table where he'd already taken a seat with his friends and Jenni was pouring his coffee. Fortunately, there were no extra chairs at that table. Unfortunately, there was an empty table for two right next to it. Jenni motioned them in that direction.

Matthew pulled a chair out for Parker. The gesture clearly startled her, but she took a seat and immediately grabbed her napkin and placed it on her lap. He remembered back. She'd always done that, and he'd always thought it kind of cute.

Brody hurried to their table, and he handed them each a menu.

"I've been promoted to waiter," Brody explained. "But only today because Carly is sick and can't come to work. Parker, did you see that baby today?"

She smiled up at him. "Not today, Brody."

His brow furrowed. "I worry about that baby's mom. Do you think she's okay?"

"I hope she is," Parker told him. "We can pray for her."

"I've been praying and we prayed at church," Brody told them. He glanced back at his mom. "I need to take your order now. Do you want coffee?"

"I would like coffee," she answered. "And I'd like an omelet."

Brody pulled the pad out of his pocket and wrote on it, his bottom lip held between his teeth as he focused. "Omelet. What about you, Matthew?"

"I'll have the French toast with bacon and hash browns."

"Got it. French toast special, omelet, two coffees." He nodded and hurried away, intent on doing the job right. All the way to the kitchen, he repeated the order to himself.

A chair scraped the floor. A moment later it settled at their table, and Kent Floyd, a lifelong resident of Sunset Ridge and a neighbor of the Rocking R, sat down. "Mind if I join you for a few?" he asked a little belatedly.

Parker arched a brow at Matthew and the look she gave him probably kept him from saying something he shouldn't, which would have been that he did mind.

"Make yourself at home," he said to the man who was only a dozen years his senior.

"Matthew, I know you've already been bothered about this, but we'd sure love to have you as a guest speaker at the church. Since we can't find a pastor to come to our small church, we like to bring in a guest speaker from time to time."

"I'm not..." he started, and the objections wouldn't come. Just then, Brody came over with their coffees, giving him a reason not to finish his thought.

He had a list of reasons to say no to Kent. What could he offer his hometown church when he wasn't even sure what he believed? How could he preach faith when his had been, sadly, shaken? He didn't want the job of pastoring Sunset Ridge Community Church. Not that they'd really offered. They wanted a guest speaker.

Across the table from him, Parker tilted her head to the side and gave him a look of encouragement.

"I know we're small potatoes for a pastor like yourself," Kent continued.

Matthew held up a hand to stop him. "It isn't that. It's just personal, Kent. I'm not sure if I can do it right now, but I'll think about it."

"Pray about it," Kent encouraged. "You know as long as you stay in town, we're probably going to keep asking. You could just get it over with."

"I know I could," Matthew agreed.

"How long are you planning to stay?" Kent asked.

"Probably through the summer." As he said it, he saw a brief flash of hurt, or something close, on Parker's face.

"I'm sure Buck is thankful to have you home."

"I think he is," Matthew said.

"I'll let you all get back to breakfast, but I'll be in

touch." With that, he stood and moved his chair back to the table of local men.

"Do you really plan to walk away from ministry?" Parker asked when they were alone.

A question many had asked, but the answer had always evaded him. He hadn't talked to anyone about the decision he had to make. He hadn't wanted to talk to anyone. At that moment, his feelings changed, because Parker sat across from him. She'd been the friend he'd talked to about life, until he'd left.

"I'm not sure if I have a plan," he admitted. "It feels wrong, to be in that church without Jared. It feels wrong to preach about faith when I'm not sure where my relationship with God stands. I'm trying to work past the moment when I realized God wasn't answering my prayers for a man who deserved to have those prayers answered."

"Maybe God answered, but it wasn't the miracle you wanted. Instead, it was the miracle of life eternal."

"Please don't say that thing about how God needed him more."

"I wouldn't dream of it," she assured him. "I don't have answers for you. I can't tell you how to feel or what to believe. I do believe that someday we will understand all of these unanswered prayers, the questions that we seem to have no answers for. I also think God can handle your anger, as long as you're seeking him for help in dealing with that anger."

Her words hit hard, because he wasn't sure he'd really taken time to pray about his anger. He'd wanted to be mad, to feel justified in walking away.

Brody appeared at just the right time to keep him

from having to answer. “I got your breakfast, Matthew. My dad said to refill your coffee.”

“That would be nice, Brody. Thank you.” Parker gave him a sweet look.

“You’re welcome, Miss Parker. My mom said you look so pretty, but you’ve always been pretty.”

“Tell her thank you.” Parker reached for the bottle of hot sauce and sprinkled it on her omelet. “This looks amazing.”

She’d always been pretty. Matthew knew that, but now, as an adult, he guessed he was seeing her a little more clearly. He saw a woman and not the girl she’d been. The girl who had laughed often, probably to hide her insecurities.

“Will you pray?” she asked Matthew.

He closed his eyes, feeling the tug of something remarkable. When her hand touched his and her fingers curled around his own, the feeling grew. He wanted to deny it, ignore it, find a way to extinguish it, but then, he also wanted to see where it would lead. It felt like hope, like a promise, and it also felt right: her hand in his as he said a blessing over their meal.

When he opened his eyes and raised his head, she looked just as startled as he felt. She opened her mouth as if to say something but then she picked up her fork and tackled her breakfast.

They were nearly finished when her phone rang. She glanced at it, ignored it for a moment and then picked it up.

“I have to take this,” she told him as she pushed her chair back from the table.

“Go ahead. I’ve got this.”

“No, I can pay for my own.” The phone continued

to ring and she gave him a quick shrug and hurried out the door.

Matthew watched her go and for a moment he wondered what he'd missed out on by not seeing her more clearly as a teenager. He'd enjoyed their friendship, but he hadn't seen how much she cared, how her laughter made him want to be a part of whatever she found amusing. He hadn't noticed the way she smelled like wildflowers and sunshine or that she had a way of making him forget himself, his seriousness.

Now that he noticed all of those things, he also realized how much he wanted to kiss her again. He knew that it would be a mistake, because they were on two different paths. The last thing he wanted was to hurt her a second time. Neither of them were in a place where a relationship made sense.

Parker felt his gaze on her as she hurried out of the café. She felt it in a physical way, the same way she'd felt the connection when they held hands during his prayer. Reaching for his hand had been a mistake.

He was a wrong turn, a road best not taken. He was the past and the past had no place in the present.

"Hello," she answered as she walked to the end of the sidewalk and then turned to overlook the park in the center of the square. It was warm, the sticky warmth of a humid summer day. Even if summer was still weeks away.

"Good morning, Parker, it's Jackie here."

"Yes," Parker breathed out, impatient to know why the caseworker had called.

"Hon, they're going to release Faith. They're thinking sometime in the next week. She's gained weight, her oxygen levels are holding and she's managing her bottles with vigor—their words."

"Oh." She didn't know what else to say. She felt a queasy feeling in the pit of her stomach.

"I have a possible long-term placement, but they're out of town for a few weeks."

Parker waited, barely breathing, her heart beating so hard she felt it echo in her ear. "I see."

"I know I'm a broken record, but I was hoping..." Jackie's voice trailed off.

"I need to think about it."

"You have a few days," Jackie said. "I'm sorry. I know I'm putting a lot of pressure on you. I wish it could all be easy. Not only your decision, but her little life and my job."

"I know," Parker said. "This isn't something I can decide right now."

"I wouldn't expect that."

Parker moved a hand to her eyes. "This is all so complicated. Jackie, can I call you tomorrow?"

"Of course you can."

She ended the call and stood there on the sidewalk, thinking about the baby girl with no one to claim her as their own. No baby should enter the world with absolutely no one to care about them.

The door behind her closed. She didn't turn, but a moment later she knew that he was there. His hand touched hers as he stepped to her side. She instantly felt comforted, maybe even stronger. He'd always been that person for her. She doubted if he had any clue what his nearness, his presence, did for her.

The idea that he made her feel whole took her by surprise. She didn't need him to be whole. She didn't need him to be happy. She didn't want to feel this way because it made her vulnerable to him.

"You okay?" he asked. "You know, you spent a lot of our teen years asking me that question. I feel I didn't reciprocate. I was pretty self-centered."

"You made me feel like I belonged here, so don't count yourself short."

"That wasn't difficult," he assured her. "But today, I can be a better friend."

She raised her gaze to him, wondering what that meant.

"Share, Parker. Tell me what's going on."

"Faith is going to be released from the hospital. Possibly this week. What am I supposed to do?"

"You're the perfect person for her, unless it isn't what you want to do." He gave her hand a squeeze. "It isn't going to be easy to make this decision. Don't let yourself be pushed into something that isn't right for you."

"I know," she said as she leaned her head against his shoulder, finding it a great comfort to have him at her side. "And in all honesty, I'm thinking of myself. I don't want to get attached and then have to leave her, or lose her. There are so many unknown variables. They could find her mom, or biological family. They could find a perfect family that can give her a forever home with two parents. And the one known variable is that I have another job in a month. I already have a condo rented with a friend."

He pulled her into a hug and held her close. She felt his lips brush the top of her head and she sighed at the way his arms around her made her feel stronger.

"I want her," she admitted in a moment of weakness,

or maybe honesty. Probably both. His arms hugged a little tighter.

"I know you do. I want her to have you."

She pulled back and wiped away the few tears that had managed to free themselves and roll down her cheeks. "This is so hard. I have work. I have a rented room. I leave soon. Should I go on with the cons?"

"Nope, I get it. What about the pros?"

She wiped away a stray tear. "Loving that little girl. The one pro is bigger than all of the cons."

"Yes, it is." He touched a strand of hair that blew across her face, gently moving it behind her ear. A look of tenderness warmed his eyes and she wanted to lean in again and feel his arms around her.

She knew that this was the road to heartache. Faith. Matthew. If only she'd taken the job in Kansas and not this job in Sunset Ridge. She'd told herself he wouldn't be here. He had his church in Chicago. A part of her, the part that seemed intent on being hurt all over again, had prayed he might come home.

So here she stood with the answer to her adult prayers, so different from those of her teen self. As an adult, she'd convinced herself that seeing him would be an opportunity for closure, for putting the past in the past.

Healing.

"I'll help you with her," he said. The words seemed to take him by surprise. The offer definitely took her by surprise.

"You what?"

"I'm here and I'm not working, I mean, other than the ranch. I can help you. And you can have my camper. It has room for one of those lacy little beds."

"A bassinet." The words slipped out. Stunned, she stood there on the sidewalk, staring up at him. It started to rain. Neither of them moved.

"Yeah, sure, bassinet." He brushed his thumb across his bottom lip, a habit he'd always had. Some things didn't change. She'd even seen him do it on broadcasts of his services.

"I don't know," she said. "It's a lot."

"Yes, it is. Pray about it." He cleared his throat. "I'm the last person that should be telling anyone to pray."

He gave a shrug and seemed boyish and uncomfortable. Her heart contracted at the sweetness of his expression and the genuine emotion behind his offer to help.

She should say no. She should make it clear that this would be a terrible idea. But he was standing there in front of her, that black cowboy hat pushed back on his head, shuffling his feet like a nervous teenager and giving off the hero vibe, the way she'd always pictured him. As her hero.

Her heart was going to break. Faith would go to a forever family and live in Parker's dream home with a fenced yard and a big dog. Matthew would go back to Chicago and she would go to her next job. They might never see each other again.

Today, though, they were here and he'd made a promise to give her what her heart longed to have, Faith in her arms and him in her life. If only for a little while.

Chapter Eight

Parker stood next to Matthew, both of them watching as Faith kicked her tiny legs and protested the hands of the pediatrician as he did a careful examination. Parker wanted to hold her, to keep her safe forever. She sensed the same feelings from Matthew, though she doubted he would admit to such strong sentiment.

Her gaze lifted to the calendar on the wall. It was the first Friday in May. Faith had been in the hospital for two weeks. All of their lives had changed in the days since finding her in the bed of Matthew's truck.

Two weeks ago, she wouldn't have considered extending her time in Sunset Ridge. She had wanted to avoid Matthew at all costs because she knew what time with him would mean to her heart, her emotions.

"She's gained weight," the doctor told them, and then he turned to the caseworker, Jackie. "She's doing well and she's ready for a home. I'm thinking by Monday she'll be ready to leave us. I'm assuming no news on family or the mother?"

Jackie shook her head. "Nothing. No one has reported

her missing, or a missing young woman who might have been pregnant."

Dr. Finley looked from Faith to Parker. "Parker, this is a big undertaking. Even if only temporarily."

"I'm aware." She continued to watch Faith. The baby now followed them with serious dark eyes. "Can I please hold her?"

"I don't see why not." Dr. Finley motioned for her to do as she pleased. She swaddled the baby and lifted her from the bed, turning as she did so that she faced Matthew.

He looked half in love. With the baby of course. He also looked scared to death. She didn't want him to feel cornered, as if he had to do this for her. She should tell him that, but not with Jackie and Dr. Finley there to witness the discussion.

Dr. Finley watched, approval in his eyes. "You managed to get a few days off at the first of the week so she can get settled in, and you can adjust to the new schedule."

"I did. I went shopping and bought what I thought we would need for a temporary stay. I'm a little nervous, but I think I can do this. With Matthew's help."

"It's a big undertaking," Jackie acknowledged. "I know you're nervous about how this will go. You're going to be great, though."

Parker closed her eyes, thinking of her verse for the day that had popped up on her phone as she drank her morning coffee. Proverbs 3:5-6. *Trust in the Lord with all thine heart; and lean not unto thine own understanding. In all thy ways acknowledge Him, and He shall direct thy paths.*

She was still unsure, but at this moment she had to

consider that Faith hadn't crossed her path by accident. In accepting that, she also accepted that God had put her on this path with Matthew. For whatever reason, He'd brought them here for this moment in their lives. Possibly for this baby. Temporarily.

Her dad had taught her many lessons on the seasons of life. He'd always warned her with each new move, "We're only here for a season. God knows what comes next."

She'd learned to accept that many friends were in her life for just a season. She had few "forever" ones and more seasonal friends.

For this season, she had Faith.

Jackie put a hand on Parker's shoulder as Parker settled into the rocking chair with the baby. "I'm going to get all of the online training set up. I did run the background checks and I'll need to get you fingerprinted. Both of you. I realize she's in Parker's custody, but if Matthew is helping, we need both."

Parker looked at the sleeping baby who was sucking her own thumb and had the warm stuffed elephant Matthew had given her tucked against her side. In her sleep, she smiled, her rosebud mouth quirking in the sweetest way. Parker's heart melted.

Jackie glanced at her watch. "I've got another appointment, but I'll catch up with you soon. I'll definitely be here Monday when you take her home and we will have a home visit."

The caseworker left and the doctor followed.

"In a little over a month, I'm supposed to move on to my next assignment," she admitted as she looked up at him, hoping to see understanding.

He nodded, getting it. "I believe in you. Don't do this

because you feel pushed to do it. Do it because it's the right thing for you and for Faith."

"Thank you," she said.

Faith moved, as if hearing them in her sleep.

Matthew smiled as he watched them together. "You're going to be a good mom. Not just for Faith, but someday when you have your own children."

Tears gathered and with her arms around the baby, she had to let them fall. She saw his brow furrow as he studied her, concern showing in his eyes.

"Parker, I'm sorry. I'm not sure what to say."

It took her a minute, but she finally found her voice and she gave him her biggest truth.

"I won't have children."

"Of course you will. You'll meet the right guy, someone decent and kind, and you'll have a family."

Her heart ached at that answer. Someone decent and kind. She wished she'd met someone that fit that description. If only she'd met a man who could have loved her for who she was and not who they wanted her to be. If only he…

She shook her head, not allowing her heart to go there.

"No, I won't. Matthew, I can't have children. Three years ago, I had a partial hysterectomy. There won't be babies. Until now, I thought I'd come to terms with my life and how things had turned out for me. I'll travel, buy a place, get a half dozen cats or so. Maybe someday I'll adopt. I hadn't considered it before, but Faith has shown me what I'm missing. Having her in my arms has been a precious gift."

He pulled her close to his side and dropped the sweetest kiss on her head. "I'm sorry."

"Me, too." She brushed a finger under her regrettably leaky eyes.

Together they both looked at the baby, now in deep sleep, her little mouth lax and one arm flopped to her side. "She is so precious."

"She is," Matthew agreed.

"I'm going to put her back in bed. She needs this sleep."

He helped her up from the rocking chair tenderly, as if she were precious to him. Her heart squeezed at the gesture and her throat felt suddenly tight. She blinked away tears that threatened to fall.

"Can I do something to help?" Matthew asked.

He meant helping with the baby, of course. She shook her head as she placed Faith in her bed, her elephant next to her. From across the room, the nurse waved. She'd been in and out of the nursery, giving them privacy and pretending she hadn't listened to their conversations.

"See you tomorrow, Parker," Hazel called out as they headed to the door.

"Yes, tomorrow." Parker gave a little wave and then exited through the door Matthew had opened for her. "I have to be on duty in an hour."

"I'm going to stop and check on Miss Philips," Matthew told her.

"I'll go with you."

Miss Philips seemed to be dozing, but as they stepped inside her room, her eyes opened and she smiled as if she'd been waiting for them.

"There you are," she said with a happy expression wreathing her face. Someone had styled her hair, and with her glasses, she seemed very focused.

"Here we are," Matthew said. "How are you today?"

"Oh, I'm fine as frog's hair. I must have been sleeping when you dropped off my glasses." She gave Matthew a wink. "How's my cat? Parker said you had a bit of a run-in."

"It was just a scratch," he assured her.

"I'm glad he's acting like his normal self. He's always been a bit of a bully. Will you read for me today? If you have time. I know I have my glasses, but your voice is very comforting."

"Psalm 91?" he asked, seeming to know what was expected of him as he took the Bible from the bedside table.

"That would be very nice, thank you." Miss Philips patted her bed and Parker took the invitation and sat next to her. A hand, thin but still strong, slipped into Parker's. "You're both very kind. I appreciate this so much."

Matthew began to read and Parker found she had to agree with Miss Philips. His voice was very comforting. As he read, she thought about the decision she needed to make concerning Faith. She'd told Jackie she could only be a temporary placement, but what if more was required? Could she stay longer than a month?

Her thoughts were racing as she considered all the possible options. Staying just long enough to find Faith a home, staying longer and possibly getting attached or raising Faith as her own. Could she be the person who adopted the infant girl?

Could she remain in Sunset Ridge?

For almost a half dozen years she'd traveled, moving from job to job every month or two. She'd been so focused on saving money to buy her own place that the lack of connections, having nowhere to call home, hadn't mattered. When she wanted home, she went to her parents. Her brother lived near them and she would just enjoy being with family.

Being a traveling nurse meant she didn't get involved. She didn't date and hadn't in a while, not since the heartbreak of taking a chance on a fellow nurse, a nice man she thought she could connect with, and then hearing those words all over again, "Parker, you're my best friend. That's all I feel for you."

She'd heard it more than once in her life.

Her gaze traveled to the man sitting in the recliner next to the bed. He'd been the first to tell her she would only ever be a friend. His words and then his walking out of her life had left scars, deep down scars.

If she stayed, she would be putting her heart on the line all over again. She would be giving her heart to the tiny baby girl who needed to be loved. She would be taking the chance that she might fall for Mathew and have her heart broken a second time when he left to return to his life in Chicago.

Matthew finished reading Psalm 91 and closed the Bible, thinking that Miss Philips had fallen asleep.

"Do you like cats, Matthew?" The elderly lady cracked one eye open.

"I'm not a fan, but I don't mind feeding Sam."

Her lips pursed as she tilted her head to the side. "Then this question will be rather awkward. Would you mind taking Sam home with you? I know that Parker can't. Erma Adams is very allergic to cats. I just don't like that Sam has been alone for so long and it looks as if it might be longer. The doctor says he's sending me to a rehabilitation facility to regain my strength. I'm quite unhappy about that because I've enjoyed our visits, and now I won't have the two of you."

Take the cat! The shock must have been evident because Miss Philips laughed just the tiniest bit and Parker arched a brow, a silent question, probably wondering how he'd get out of this.

"I…" He didn't know what to say.

"I understand it's a lot to ask. If I had anyone else, I wouldn't be asking."

"I know you wouldn't. The problem is that I'm not sure how long I'll be in Sunset Ridge."

"Oh goodness, I don't plan on being gone for months. You haven't said much, but I assume you're taking a little time away from the ministry?"

"I am. I'm here to help my dad and to make sure he's physically able to take care of the ranch."

"And to make peace with God." She gave him a knowing look.

"Yes, and that." Matthew reached for her hand. "I'll take Sam to my place, but only until you're on your feet again. And, Miss Philips, I'll visit you if you'll give me the name of the facility."

"I'd like that very much." She pointed to a brochure on the table next to her bed. "That's the place. It's here in Wagoner."

"Do you know when they'll be moving you?"

"Probably at the first of the week."

"I'll stop by your place and get your cat. I'll take good care of him."

"I know you will."

They walked out of her room, but Matthew found he couldn't walk away from his concern for her. It seemed that even leaving the ministry, he couldn't shed the person he'd been for the past dozen years. It was a part of him.

"You're very quiet," Parker said as they walked down the hall toward the exit.

"Just thinking about Miss Philips, and ministry."

"I see."

He slowed his pace. "Is that all you have to say? No words of wisdom?"

"None," she said, her dimples flashing and her eyes sparkling with humor. "I'm the last person to try and tell you what you're supposed to be doing with your life since my master plan seems to be full of plot holes."

His hand slid into hers and they finished the walk down the hall, hand in hand.

"I have to go to work," she said. "And you have to go look at the Jackson house."

"I do. You know, once I close on the place, you could live there with Faith. It's definitely roomier than the camper."

He'd taken her to the camper the previous day, after they'd made the trip to look at the cattle he planned to buy. It had been a full day that had also included a trip to a discount store for baby items. He couldn't deny that it had been strange, buying all of those things with Parker. One cashier had even asked the age of their baby. Theirs. As in the two of them. Together.

They stopped at the door to the ER.

"I think the camper will be fine. No need for me to move into a bigger place and then have to move again."

He felt an odd pain to the chest as he thought about her leaving. Regret? Missing her already? Regret because he'd long ago walked away from her friendship and he hadn't really looked back. Missing her because now he knew the hole she'd left.

What if he hadn't laughed off her declaration of love? If they'd taken a different path, they might have been standing there as partners in life, considering the very real chance that Faith might be in their lives forever.

He wasn't that person, though. He wasn't the man who had ever allowed himself to think about marriage and family. He'd watched marriage wreck his parents, his siblings and even himself.

Remaining single had fit his life. As a single minister, he didn't have to feel guilty about leaving his home in the middle of the night, spending hours with a sick church member or a family in crisis. He'd given 100 percent of himself to his ministry, to his congregation.

He cleared his throat, uncomfortable with those thoughts and all of the emotion that went along with them. "Anyway, the camper or the house, either is yours for as long as you want."

She stood on tiptoe to kiss his cheek. "Thank you. For being in this journey with me, for your camper and for the offer of a home."

She was adorable with her sweet smile and golden-brown eyes.

"You're welcome," he told her as he stepped away. "I'll see you tomorrow."

She nodded and then she hurried through the door. He walked back down the hall. He'd parked outside the main entrance. Walking this direction meant he'd go past the nursery. Maybe he'd slip in and see Faith before he headed back to the ranch.

He had to admit, she was growing on him. He'd never thought much about babies, other than the ones he'd held and prayed for when their parents brought them to church for a dedication to the Lord. He had never considered having children. They hadn't even been a "someday, down the road" thought. Faith, with her dark eyes and downy soft hair, changed things for him.

"Mr. Rivers. Hello. Do you have a minute?"

Matthew slowed his steps and glanced back, waiting for Chaplain Rogers to catch up with him. The older man picked up his pace and joined him.

"How can I help you?" Matthew asked as they walked down the hall together. He bypassed the nursery with a quick look in that direction.

Chaplain Rogers's expression changed from serious to mirthful.

"You might wish you hadn't asked," the older man said with a grin. "I have a favor to ask. Before I do, just know that I realize this is a lot and I understand if it is too much."

Matthew felt a knot of tension in his gut, in anticipation of whatever the minister might be on the verge of saying. "Okay," he said, and he sounded fairly calm and open.

"I've given this a lot of prayer and it isn't easy to ask, but you're the person who kept coming to mind."

Matthew remained quiet and gave just a quick nod to encourage the other man. He pushed the doors open and they exited the building together. Clouds had rolled in and a light breeze blew, the kind of breeze that turned the leaves and hinted at rain.

"Do you mind if we continue our walk?" Chaplain Rogers asked. "It's easier to talk and walk."

"I agree," Matthew said.

So they walked, and yet, Chaplain Rogers didn't talk.

Instead, he strolled with his hands behind his back and his features reflecting that he had much on his mind. Matthew waited.

"My wife isn't well," Chaplain Rogers said after several minutes. "I'm the pastor, the chaplain, the man of God. Who does the pastor go to when he needs to be ministered to?"

"Another pastor," Matthew offered, even though he wasn't sure he could still call himself a pastor. Did a pastor have a lot of regrets and more doubts?

This time last year, he would have gone to Jared. The thought brought a mixed-up flash of pain and anger that nearly made him miss what the man next to him had to say. At the moment, Chaplain Rogers needed for Matthew to be the man he went to, the person he confided in.

"I'd appreciate prayer. We're going to Tulsa for treatments and it's going to be a battle, but the prognosis is good."

Pray. It was a simple request and yet, the words brought memories of the day Jared had been taken by the ambulance. He'd seemed fine and he'd told Matthew to pray and to call his wife. Matthew hadn't thought a thing about that prayer. In the coming days, the prayers had changed and he'd pleaded with God to save his friend, his partner in ministry.

He shook loose from the thoughts and managed to say the words the other man needed to hear.

"I'll pray for you both. And is there anything else I can do for you?"

Chaplain Rogers stopped walking. "I'm going to take a leave of absence from my work here at the hospital."

"That's understandable," Matthew said. "You need to be with your wife."

"She's my priority. I serve Him and Him alone, but He gave me a wonderful wife to love and protect. I think He'll understand that I need to be with her now."

They were walking again, this time in the direction of the parking lot. There was more that Chaplain Rogers needed to ask. Matthew could see it in his expression, in the way he walked with his hands behind his back, deep in thought.

"Matthew, there's one more thing I'd like to ask you."

"What is it?"

"Could you fill in for me here at the hospital? They need a chaplain. It would only be temporary. The idea of leaving my patients with no one to turn to is a burden."

The request brought him up short. He didn't have the words to convey how much he did not want the job of chaplain, how lacking he felt for the position. He couldn't stand before the people of Sunset Ridge Community Church and preach a sermon on faith, or tell the patients at this hospital to have faith if he didn't know where he stood on the subject.

When he didn't respond immediately, Chaplain Rogers went on. "I'm sorry, maybe I was wrong in asking you. I just felt like you were the man for the job. You've been so kind to Miss Philips and I've seen you step in and speak to other patients as you made your way to see baby Faith."

Matthew shook his head, not in disagreement with the chaplain but just to clear his thoughts. "Chaplain Rogers, I'll be honest, I'm home to figure out what I'm going to do with my life. I'm not sure if I'm even called to ministry."

Chaplain Rogers gave him a gentle smile. "Matthew, you can be angry and you can question God, but that doesn't mean your faith is gone. It just needs to be replenished."

Not me, Lord. Isn't that what Moses had said? *Not me.* Jonah had said the same thing. Both men, and so many more throughout history, had told God to send someone else, someone more qualified, someone less broken.

Matthew had struggled for six months. He'd dwelled in his anger, his bitterness, his mourning for his friend. He wasn't sure if he could let go and step into a role of ministry.

"I'm going to have to think about this."

"I understand," Chaplain Rogers responded. "I know it's a lot to ask. You didn't come here to take on a ministry."

No, he'd come here running from ministry. Instead, he'd been bombarded by folks at the Sunset Ridge Community Church, a ministry that badly needed a minister. Now this. Looking at Chaplain Rogers, he found it difficult to say no.

He found it harder to say yes.

"I don't need an answer today, but would you pray about it?"

"I will."

They parted, and he took the long way home to Sunset Ridge, driving on back roads that ran past large farms, some dotted with oil pumps. Country music played on the radio and he rolled down the window, letting warm air blow through the cab of the truck. In the distance, those promising rain clouds darkened the sky and the branches of the trees swirled in the wind.

His father, Parker, Faith, Miss Philips and now the chaplain. He thought about each of them and what they needed. It felt more like talking than praying, but he thought it counted as prayer.

He'd come home in an attempt to run from God. It seemed God had chased him all the way to Oklahoma.

He'd chased him right back to his past. Now Matthew had to figure out what to do with that past. Parker—he pictured her pretty face, her incredible eyes. She'd been a part of the past, a friend and then not a friend, but a girl who thought she might love him.

Now they were tied together in a way neither of them could have expected, by a tiny baby girl named Faith.

Chapter Nine

Faith's going home day didn't happen until Wednesday of the next week, five days after the doctor predicted. She'd fought a stomach ailment, running a low-grade fever and losing precious ounces. Matthew arrived at the hospital early that afternoon and met up with Parker. She'd worked that morning, so she still wore her pale blue scrubs, the ones with teddy bears. Her smile trembled nervously, and her eyes were glistening.

"Is something wrong?" he asked, fighting the urge to gather her in his arms and hold her.

She shook her head. "Nothing. Just worried that I'm the wrong person for this."

"I don't think there could be anyone better for this little girl than you. Even if it is temporary, you're perfect."

"I'm not perfect," she said, her gaze averted. He wanted her to look at him, so he could convince her that she could do this.

He remained quiet, knowing that she had more on her mind than the baby, probably more than her eventual departure. He reached for her hand and linked theirs together, his fingers through hers. She glanced up, her brown eyes searching and troubled.

"Matthew, I'm going to be honest. I'm not sure why you're here with me. You don't have to be involved in caring for this baby. You didn't have to give me your place. I'm trying very hard not to..." She glanced away and she didn't finish what she'd planned on saying. "I missed you for a long time. I don't want to miss you again."

With her thumb and finger, she pinched the bridge of her nose. Matthew stepped close, glad they were alone in the hallway. Gently he placed a kiss on the top of her head, inhaling the scent of wildflowers. For just a moment, she rested her cheek on his shoulder.

"I want you to be able to take Faith, even if it's temporary." He realized that didn't sound like a real answer. "I want to help you. I can't explain, because there doesn't seem to be an explanation. It just seems like one of those situations that neither of us can run from?"

"And we've both done our share of running," she said with a glimpse of humor reflected in her eyes.

"We're definitely skilled at running. Me more so than you." He glanced in the direction of the chapel. "Chaplain Rogers is taking a leave of absence."

"I'd heard."

"He asked if I would fill in a few days a week. Temporarily, of course."

She actually giggled. "What did you tell him?"

"I told him I'm the wrong person, but that I'd pray."

"You'd make an excellent chaplain," she said as she pushed the button to access the nursery. "Unless you're still running?"

"I'm not running. I'm evaluating my life and my future."

Again, she laughed. "Okay, keep telling yourself that."

They entered the nursery. Jackie, the caseworker, had arrived ahead of them. She held Faith, talking to the baby girl, now dressed in her going home outfit. Dr. Finley and two of the nurses who'd helped care for her were also there. They'd printed a banner and tied together balloons to make an arch over the door. It had the makings of a farewell party and, if he had to guess, there would be tears.

"Are the two of you ready for this?" Jackie asked as she handed over Faith in her floral dress that Parker had picked out the day they went shopping.

"We are," Parker responded. "Though, I'm going to be honest, I'm worried. What if I can't do it? What if I mess up?"

"You have people to call," Jackie reminded her. "You have a support system. First, you have Matthew. You have me. You said your mother is onboard and will be a phone call away. We're all here, available if you need to talk. Matthew will be a two minute walk from you, or you from him. Since it seemed unlikely that parents are going to appear out of thin air, it's a blessing that you're able to take her."

"Have you heard anything on the investigation?" Matthew asked. It never left his mind for long: the thought that somewhere out there was a mom who had chosen to abandon her baby girl. He wondered if she was safe, or if she needed help.

"I think they have some leads," Jackie said. "The local dollar store reported seeing a young girl, maybe seventeen or eighteen and pregnant. She stopped coming in to shop and when they asked her friend about her, the girl got nervous and took off. They haven't seen either since talking to the friend."

"So, they might have left the area?" Parker asked, her voice catching with emotion.

"That's the assumption," Jackie said as she handed Faith to Parker. "Here you go, Mama."

At the word "Mama," Parker's eyes overflowed with tears. She brought the baby close and sniffled as the tears rolled down her cheeks.

Matthew searched the room until he found a box of tissues. He stood there, not sure if he should wipe her eyes since she held the baby. Or could she wipe them? A watery giggle broke them free from the heavy emotions and she took the tissues from his hand.

"Whatever you do, Matthew Rivers, do not try to hold that up to my nose and tell me to blow."

"I considered it."

"I could tell you were thinking about it." She wiped her eyes. "Ugh, this is tough."

"You know how to take care of her," Dr. Finley said. "She is little, but healthy. The heart murmur is something her pediatrician will keep an eye on. She's going to need extra patience and love. These babies have a different path. She was born early, traumatically, and addicted to drugs. It's hard to imagine having to start life with those obstacles, but you're going to sing to her, read to her and pray for her. She's going to do great things."

Parker kissed the baby's dark head and then she placed her in the new infant carrier. As she buckled the baby in, she explained the process to Matthew. "In case you ever need to do this. She did really great yesterday when they tested her in the car seat to make sure her oxygen levels remained stable."

He hadn't been able to make it to the hospital the previous day. He'd taken his father to a doctor's appointment in Tulsa, a specialist who insisted Buck needed knee replacement surgery. Buck had argued and left in the middle of the examination. He'd promptly called his daughter, Jael, to tell her what he thought of the specialist she'd recommended. Matthew had felt sorry for the sister he really didn't know all that well. She'd been born after Izzy left her husband and sons.

Another mom who had left her children behind—Matthew's own mother. He'd been the lone sibling who'd gone to counseling, confronting those feelings of abandonment. This baby wouldn't remember being abandoned, but the trauma would still affect her life.

"Ready to go?" Parker asked after tucking a lightweight blanket around the baby. She had a backpack with supplies. He took it from her, but she held on to the handle of the infant seat.

"I'm ready," he said. "Are you?"

She nodded, her gaze lowering to the baby in the seat and her eyes taking on a misty, tender look. A maternal look.

Jackie gave them a few last-minute instructions and a time when she'd be coming by to check in on them. And then they were going down the hall together, looking for all the world like a family leaving the hospital with their newborn.

How would Parker let go when it was time to leave? Matthew had no idea, because he could see for himself that letting go wouldn't be easy. Not this time around.

* * *

Parker picked up the infant carrier with the baby strapped snugly and safely inside. Matthew reached to take it from her.

"Do you want me to carry her?"

She had hold of the carrier and she couldn't let go, not with Faith studying her intently with her dark eyes.

"It isn't heavy, just awkward."

He nodded and gave her an understanding look. "If you change your mind."

"I'll let you know."

She needed the baby to hold on to. The carrier *was* heavy, but it was real and grounded her in a moment when she needed that. She'd called her parents the previous evening to talk this decision over with them. They always listened and gave only the necessary advice. She appreciated that they would let her talk out her feelings.

They approved of the decision to take Faith on a temporary basis. They also knew that this would make leaving more difficult. She wondered if they were hoping that Faith would ground her and keep her in one place for a while.

Matthew's hand moved to her back, the touch supportive and comforting. "You're going to be great at this."

"I hope so," she answered. "It's frightening and exciting, all at the same time."

"I agree. It is. I'm not even the one doing the real work."

"You're going to be more help than you realize."

She glanced up at the man walking next to her, her partner in this undertaking. He'd changed to a white cowboy hat, probably due to the warm weather. He walked with confidence, the way he always had. Tall and broad-shouldered, as if he could handle anything that came his way. He gave her a quick grin, the gesture settling her, making her feel grounded.

They had arrived at her car and he took the keys from her hand and opened the back door for her. "I'll get it started so it can be cooling off."

"Thank you," she told him as she leaned to put the seat in the back, rear facing and snapped into the base. She tested to make sure it was stable.

As she stepped back to close the door, she realized Matthew had come and stood behind her, so close she could smell the cologne he wore, so different from the body spray the boys had worn in high school. He smelled expensively of cedar, sage and other earthy fragrances. His arm encircled her and he pulled her to his side.

"She's going to be fine." The deep timbre of his voice soothed, but also had her sinking into him a bit more.

His hand slid to her waist. She moved away, needing space and hoping he didn't think it was due to him, his touch. It was her and the twenty pounds she still wanted to lose. She would never be thin, but she would be healthy and she was happy with herself.

So why did his touch bring back all of the old insecurities?

He studied her as she got in the driver's seat, obviously waiting for a response to what he'd said about Faith. "I know she'll be fine. Will I?" The last part, she hadn't meant to say.

Compassion darkened his eyes and he shrugged. "You will, because you're strong and you know Who you are trusting in."

"Thank you for that reminder. I'll see you at the Rocking R." She reached to close the door.

He leaned in and surprised her with a sweet and swift kiss on her cheek. "You're a hero."

And then he backed away and closed the door softly but firmly. She watched him walk across the parking lot to his truck before she backed out and drove away. He would meet her, so she didn't have long to pull herself together, to put her emotions firmly in place.

By the time she reached the ranch, she'd given herself a firm talking to and she believed in her ability to resist Matthew, his charm, his kindness, his kisses. She pulled down the driveway, and she parked next to the camper he normally called home.

He'd given it up for her. She knew it wouldn't be easy for him to stay in the house with Buck. Maybe it would help the two of them, father and son, to find a path to healing.

She got out of her car and Matthew was there, already opening the door and pulling out the bags that needed to be taken inside. She craned her neck to look up at him, shading her eyes with her hand.

"I should have asked sooner," she said as a thought came to her. "What about Miss Philips's cat, Sam? Is he in that camper?"

"No. I moved him to the house with Dad. They seem to get along."

"I bet they do."

He hefted the backpack diaper bag over his shoulder and stepped back to give her room.

"I made sure the air is on, the bassinet is ready and the fridge is stocked," he told her.

"You've thought of everything. Why is it you're not married with a family?"

"You already know the answer to that question."

"You still worry that you would end up with a broken family, following in the footsteps of your parents? I think you know that isn't who you are."

"It started that way, but I think over time the reasons changed," he said. "I found that being single gave me more opportunity to serve the people in the church and the community. I didn't have to feel torn between serving the church and serving a wife and children."

"People balance ministry and family," she said as she unbuckled the car seat and pulled it from the base to carry it inside.

"Most do," he agreed.

"My dad always managed to be there for us, but also for our church. It's a juggling act, for sure."

"I haven't had to juggle," he admitted. "I liked it that way."

"We should get her inside," she told him, needing to shift gears and not think about him and his new reasons for not marrying. She didn't need one more reason why. "She's starting to wake up. Any minute now, she'll realize she's hungry."

She wasn't wrong about the swift transition. They were barely inside when Faith let out a pitiful cry, bringing all the volume as she grew impatient with waiting for her bottle.

"If you get her out of the seat," Parker said, watching as he tried to comfort the baby.

He worked at the buckle, eyes narrowed as he concentrated on the clasp. It was endearing to watch the big strong man, cowboy hat pushed back and his large hands, trying so hard to unfasten the five-pound baby from her seat. He caught her watching.

"What's so funny?" he asked with a flash of white teeth, a dimple materializing in his cheek.

"Not funny," she explained. "Well, maybe a little bit funny. Definitely sweet."

An infusion of red colored his cheeks. Gah, she needed to turn away now. The combination of an embarrassed and adorable man holding a tiny baby girl might be too much for any woman's heart. Unfortunately, in the small confines of the camper, putting space between them proved impossible. The kitchen took up most of one wall. The living area was just opposite. The adorable cowboy holding the baby girl took up a lot of room in that small area.

He held the baby against his shoulder, comforting her and then singing to her when rubbing her back didn't work. Parker turned and kept her head down as she poured water into the bottle and then added the recommended scoops of formula. Matthew continued to sing. He'd always had a beautiful voice and it had only improved with age. Faith's cries quieted to a whimper.

"Here we go." Parker held out the bottle.

"You should probably feed her," he said, handing the swaddled infant over.

"Are you sure?"

"I'm very sure."

Parker offered Faith the bottle and then she took a seat. The baby sucked the bottle greedily. It was the sweetest and possibly most profound moment of Parker's life. She might not—no, she *wouldn't*—marry and have children, but for the moment she could have

Faith. She could pour love into the tiny infant who had no one else.

"What next?" Matthew asked. "I'm going to admit, I'm pretty lost now that we've left the safety of the hospital."

"She's fine, Matthew. I'll feed her, change her diaper, cuddle her a bit and then put her down to sleep." The bedroom of the camper was small, but it fit the bassinet perfectly.

Matthew leaned against the counter and watched her feed the baby. "I should go."

"You don't have to leave. I'm not going to rush you out the door."

"I know, but I have things I should probably do. Dad has another doctor's appointment next week. I'm trying to clean up some of the fence rows before then. They're overgrown with weeds and trees."

"No matter what the situation, you kept this place up as a teen. You and your brothers."

"They didn't always appreciate that," he shared. "They would have been happy to sell the place."

"And you?"

"There were times I felt the same way. And yet, here I am back at home trying to save it. I don't want to live here, but I can't sit back and watch the family farm get sold on the courthouse steps."

"You might decide to stay."

He chuckled at that. "It would be a cold day for that to happen."

"Have you decided what to do about the chaplain position?" she asked, knowing it was time to change the subject. Probably, the chaplain position wasn't the best change.

He pulled off his cowboy hat, but he held it in his hand, absently looking it over.

"I'm considering it," he said after a bit. "I know it's going to be tough, but then that's putting myself and my feelings first. I want to help the people like Miss Philips, the ones who are alone and need a comforting word, someone to talk to, someone who cares."

"It won't be easy," Parker agreed. "But I think you're the right person for the job. You do care. It's genuine and people respond to that."

"Thank you for saying that. I'm not sure where I'm going after this, but I know that if I go back to ministry, I need to know without a doubt that I'm called. I can't stand behind a pulpit and tell people to have faith if I don't have that same faith."

"You know that people can have a faith crisis and it doesn't mean they've stopped believing," she said softly, not wanting to wake the baby. "Maybe it isn't my place to say, but I think your struggle proves that your faith is real. You were angry. God says to be angry and don't sin. He doesn't say that we can't ever be angry."

"I expected Him to heal Jared." He lowered his gaze to study the infant. "The effectual fervent prayer of a righteous man?"

"Now we see through a glass darkly," she paraphrased. "Someday we will understand in full."

"Someday," he agreed. He shoved his hat back on his head. "Buck said to invite you down for supper. I told him I'll invite you, but you choose when you're ready for that."

"Buck cooks?"

"That's what he says. I guess we'll find out."

"Maybe in a day or two, if the invitation is open."

"I'm sure it will be." He knelt next to her, touching Faith's tiny hand and smiling when the infant stretched and then curled up again. "She's perfect."

"Fearfully and wonderfully made," Parker agreed. "I hope she always believes that about herself."

"I hope so, too. It isn't always easy to see our own beauty." The way he said it made her look up, trying to figure out what he meant. She couldn't help it. She was a woman and she wondered what he saw when he looked at her.

It had taken her years to believe in her own beauty. There were still times when she looked in the mirror and she felt her fifteen-year-old self rising up to taunt her, telling her she was overweight and her clothes were out of style.

She often reminded herself that God made her in His image and that meant the part of her that cared about others, the part that was kind, the part that served others, that was the person who was created in His image. God created her, and what she saw as flaws or the things that needed to be changed, He saw as His creation. If He loved that creation, she should love herself.

Matthew had been studying her and now he pushed to his feet. With a swiftness that didn't give her time to think, he leaned in and kissed her. His mouth captured hers, tender and sweet, his hand cupping her cheek.

"You are beautiful," he said softly as he pulled away and then left the camper, leaving her to deal with the fallout of her emotions, her brain scrambling to understand how he could say something like that and walk away.

He would break her heart. As sure as the wind blew in Oklahoma, when he left, he would take a piece of her heart with him. She should have learned her lesson the first time around. She obviously hadn't learned anything, or she would have steered clear of Matthew Rivers.

Chapter Ten

Matthew couldn't escape the cat. It had been two days since Parker moved into the camper with Faith, while the cat and Matthew had moved into the house with Buck. The cat rubbed against his legs, climbed in his bed and thought the refrigerator was his personal throne.

"Get, Sam." Matthew moved the cat off the counter as he filled the animal's food bowl. "Go on."

"Talking to the cat again?" Buck asked as he entered the kitchen.

"If you'd go to the doctor, you might not need that cane for the rest of your life," Matthew said, nodding to the wooden cane his dad had found in a closet.

"I don't need no doctor to tell me my joints are getting old. And if you're here in Oklahoma just to nag at me and try to get me to have surgery, you can go back to Chicago." Buck narrowed his eyes and gave Matthew a long look. "Is that baby strapped to your—" he stopped himself from cursing "—to your chest?"

"She is," he admitted, looking down at the little girl sleeping soundly in the strange contraption wrapped around his middle and his neck.

Buck shook his head and poured himself a cup of coffee. "I ain't never seen the like."

"I'm sure you haven't." Matthew moved the conversation to neutral ground before Buck gave him a lecture about the differences between men and women. "I made you an omelet."

"I want cookies and milk."

"You're cantankerous," Matthew said. "And you're not in kindergarten, so cookies and milk are out. Eat your omelet. It'll keep your blood sugar levels more stable."

"I didn't need you to come home and nurse me." Buck grabbed the plate and hobbled to the table. "How's the baby? You were down there pretty late last night."

"As you can see, she's good. She was a little on the fussy side yesterday."

"Where's Parker?" Buck asked.

"Working. They were short-staffed."

"You should marry that gal and make a family with her and that baby."

"I'm not marrying anyone." It felt a little harder to say when "that baby" was strapped to his chest, her dark eyes peering up at him, content and loved.

"So you say. Did I hear you telling that chaplain that you're thinking you might take his job at the hospital? I thought you were done with preaching?"

"Being a chaplain is about giving comfort, not preaching sermons. Also, it's only temporary."

Did Buck look disappointed? Oh well, he was used to seeing disappointment in his father's eyes.

"Different sides of the same coin," his dad said as he dug into the omelet. "When are those cows being delivered? And are you taking that baby down there? Is that safe?"

Matthew glanced at his watch. "Thirty minutes. Yes, I'm taking her. Yes, it'll be safe. I won't let her get hurt and I have a flap to keep the sun off her. I'm going to put on my work boots. I'll meet you down there, since you obviously aren't going to stay inside."

"No, I'm not staying inside. It's still my ranch."

"Fine, yes, it is still your ranch."

"But thank you for paying the taxes."

"You're welcome. I'll meet you at the barn." He saluted with a cup of coffee and then he left the room. Neither he nor his father needed messy, emotional words about the ranch staying in the family.

Matthew slipped into his work boots and headed out the back door of the house, knowing that as he closed the door, the cat had jumped up in the window to watch. He wasn't about to admit that he liked the animal. The sooner he left this place, the better off he'd be. He had to remind himself daily that he didn't like cats, the country or babies.

It was getting hard to remember why he didn't like those things, or if it had ever been the truth.

The baby nestled against his chest made him a liar when it came to children. He liked her. A lot. He put a hand to her back and rubbed gently, knowing from the soft, regular breathing that she'd gone back to sleep. The fierce protectiveness he felt for five pounds of humanity took him by surprise.

A truck and trailer rattled up the driveway before pulling to a stop at the barn. Inside the trailer he could see the shimmering cream coats of the Charolais cows he'd bought. Last week he'd purchased a bull, and now the animal—over a ton of muscle and attitude—approached the fence to watch his new harem and wait for them to be unloaded.

None of this felt like the path to leaving this place, to returning to his life, his career. His ministry. He pushed his hat back and motioned the truck back, waving his hand until the vehicle got close enough to the gate for them to unload the cattle.

From the corral, a horse whinnied. A cutting horse he'd bought from a longtime friend. Another mistake, that horse?

Maybe he never intended to leave? Maybe he'd come home thinking to put down roots and finish the book he'd started this past winter, the work that he hadn't touched since Jared's death. *Journey to Faith* had been the tentative title. The irony of that hadn't been lost on him. Even if he finished, it would never be the book he'd planned to write.

Faith now meant a tiny baby girl, Parker's smile and the journey that baby had taken them on. Through that little child, Matthew thought he might be learning new lessons on trust, on acceptance. Maybe the book really would be her story.

He shook loose from all those thoughts and watched as Jerry, nearly as old as Buck, wiry and bowlegged, jumped out of his truck and headed Matthew's way. He had a big smile and an honest streak as wide as the Mississippi. Matthew joined him at the gate.

Jerry gave him a long look and shook his head. "You got a baby in that pouch?"

"I do," he admitted again with a grin sneaking up on him.

Jerry got close and peeked in, whistling softly.

"Mighty pretty little girl. Mighty sad way to start her life. We've had her on the church prayer list."

"Thank you."

"Can you do this with her strapped to you that way?"

"I guess I can. We've gotten pretty used to this. She goes with me to feed cattle and she is a pretty good hand when it comes to keeping Buck out of trouble."

Jerry laughed at that. "Stay there. I'll get the gates. Wouldn't want one of these girls getting sideways on you and that baby."

Jerry swung the back of the stock trailer open. The cows stood huddled in the back of the trailer, not quite ready to greet the handsome bull who bellowed a greeting. Jerry went to the back of the trailer. Matthew went to the other side. They managed to get the cows moving out of the trailer and into the field. Buck hurried forward to close the gate, grimacing as he did, but then covering the look with a whistle of appreciation.

"Mighty fine-looking animals," Buck said as he came to stand next to Matthew. He leaned hard on the top rail of the fence. "Those aren't the kind of cattle a man buys if he's only staying for a few months."

"I bought them for you," Matthew said, ignoring the rush of guilt because he'd just been saying the same thing to himself. What was he doing buying livestock for this place? They were still rebuilding fences and he'd just called a contractor to give him a bid on barn repairs.

"They'll sure improve the livestock we've got." Buck glanced at the other man as he raised a booted foot to rest it on the lower rail of the wood fence. "What do you think, Jerry?"

Jerry didn't have to say what he thought. He'd raised

these cattle and he knew their breeding. Also, Jerry didn't typically say much.

"Guess they'll do."

Matthew hid a grin at the comment. For what he'd paid, they'd better do.

"What happened to your hat?" Buck asked, taking a sidestep to study Matthew's favorite hat. Jerry's attention caught and he also gave the hat a good long look before shaking his head in disbelief.

"Sam," Matthew said, grinding his teeth.

"The cat?" Buck chuckled as he asked.

"The cat," Matthew confirmed. "He jumped off the counter, knocked the hat off the hook and proceeded to attack it."

The entire hat looked chewed up and it had long snags from the cat's claws. Matthew had come to the conclusion that the cat was some kind of punishment. Jonah had been tossed into the sea and swallowed by a giant fish.

Matthew had inherited, for the time being, a cat with claws.

Faith moved a bit, her tiny hand clutching at the cloth of the carrier holding her close to him. It had a fancy name. He called it his kangaroo pouch. He rubbed a hand lightly over her head and spoke to her in a soft, and hopefully reassuring voice.

When he looked up, both men were watching him.

Buck took a step away from the fence but immediately reached for it again. Matthew shot him a questioning look that Buck ignored.

Jerry cleared his throat.

"Matthew, I know you've been asked before," Jerry started. Matthew immediately knew where the conversation would go. "But I'd sure like it if you'd consider preaching on Sunday morning. It's my week and God knows I'm not a speaker or a preacher. I know it would do the entire congregation a lot of good to hear from someone else. They've grown a little stagnant since we haven't had a minister. The younger families are leaving and the older folks are giving up."

Matthew pictured Jonah telling God he wasn't going to Nineveh and then boarding a boat that he thought would take him away from all his troubles. It had taken a storm, being cast overboard and then swallowed by a giant fish to get Jonah's attention.

Well, he wasn't Jonah and Sunset Ridge wasn't Nineveh. Matthew opened his mouth to tell Jerry he couldn't. Wouldn't.

"Okay." Came out.

He shook his head again. Preach? About what? About being angry with God and doubting his own faith, his call to ministry? He hadn't stood behind a pulpit in six months.

Just be honest, Parker had told him. *People sometimes doubt, they get angry, so be honest about how you feel.*

He started to say something, probably to tell Jerry he'd made a mistake and couldn't do it. At that moment, Buck took a step and crumpled. Jerry and Matthew both reached for him, and they brought him back to his feet.

"Dratted knee," Buck muttered. "Let me go and I'll be fine."

"You're not fine," Matthew told his father. "I'm taking you to the emergency room."

"Now how do you plan on forcing me?" Buck probably tried to snarl but it came out with a grimace attached.

"Since you obviously can't run from me, and you can't walk out of the office like you did last time, I think I'll win this battle."

Jerry helped him get Buck to the truck. The whole time, Faith snuggled in close, her eyes open and watching his face. He knew that Parker worried about the heartache attached with someday having to let go of that baby girl. He would also have to say good-bye to Parker. He realized then that he might not be as good at letting go as he had been all those years ago.

Parker finished the salad she'd brought for lunch, tossed her trash and packed away the containers. It had been a long day and she wanted to go home. She wanted to hold Faith close and cuddle her while the baby took her evening bottle.

She wanted to see Matthew.

She shook her head at the thought. She didn't need to see him. They'd texted periodically throughout the day. Each time she'd seen his name on her phone, she'd gotten excited at the prospect of hearing from him.

Or maybe she had been excited to hear a little about Faith's day—to receive a picture of her.

Her name over the intercom caught her attention. She paused in the hall to listen, thinking it might have been someone else. Nope, the call came again for her to return to the emergency room. She knew it could be anything—she worked in the ER and it made sense that if they'd gotten overrun, they might call her back—but something made her fear it was a personal, not work-related summons. She ran, her heart racing as fast as her feet, fear tightening her throat. Something must have happened to Faith. Her heart felt ready to beat out of her chest and her lungs burned. She rushed through the doors.

Matthew stood in the brightly lit central hall of the ER, Faith snug against his chest. He smiled as if he hadn't scared ten years off her life.

"Hey, that was quick." He said it with a grin.

"I thought it was Faith. You scared the life out of me."

His eyes widened and then he shook his head. "Oh, Parker, no. It's my dad and his knee. He hurt it this morning and he collapsed on me. I had them call you in case I need to help with Buck."

She closed her eyes and drew in a few deep breaths. "I'm going to hurt you."

His arm came around her and he pulled her close to his side. The comfort there, next to him, took her by surprise. She didn't want to need anyone, most of all him, but there were these moments when it felt as if she'd been waiting for him her entire life.

Those thoughts were followed by the others—the warning thoughts: how it felt to be left, how it felt to be a friend with no hope of being more.

"Give her to me," she said. "I'll feed her and change her."

"I'm glad you said that, because a few minutes ago she really started to stink." He told her this as he handed the baby over, not giving her a chance to back away.

"This isn't fair." But she couldn't help but smile, first at Faith and then Matthew. "But I'll take diaper duty so you can be with your father."

"Wait, maybe I want to change that diaper," he teased. His eyes sparkled with humor and then… She drew in a breath. And then something else, something deeper and warmer that gave her comfort and a feeling of peace. Something that could make a girl wish for a happy ending.

"Nope, you made your choice." And she'd made hers. She hurried off, tucking away any emotions that shouldn't have room in her heart or life.

When she returned from changing the diaper, she found Matthew with Buck. She listened at the door as the two talked.

"Buck, I don't understand why you won't have the surgery. I can't imagine that you want to stay in pain for the rest of your life."

"What does it matter to you?" Buck shot back at him. "You're still calling me Buck."

A long pause followed.

"Okay, Dad. It matters because I want you to be healthier."

"So you can leave," Buck grumbled. "Why did I ever quit drinking?"

"Because you were tired of that life?"

"No, because I listened to a few of my son's sermons. And then I went to that church in town. I heard the bells ringing and I thought, why not? I went once, thinking I'd give it a shot and then I went back again and again. And I realized that I'd been filling up this empty hole in my life with bottle after bottle of whiskey, but the hole never filled up. It was a God-sized hole that only He could fill."

Parker watched Matthew come to terms with what faith had meant to his father. The same faith he'd been running from. There was a moment when the look could only be described as grief.

"I'm glad you found the answer," Matthew said quietly, and then he sighed. "We were discussing your need for surgery."

Buck waved his gnarled hand. "I'm not having the surgery."

"Why?" Parker asked, stepping into the room.

Buck heaved a sigh, too. "Well, I guess because the recovery time is weeks, months, I don't know. I don't have time for no rehab facility. Now you've bought cattle and horses, plus the Jackson place. How am I supposed to take care of all that nonsense by myself if I'm laid up? You've made it clear you're not going to be here." He glanced at Parker, for some reason including her. "And you'll be gone soon."

"I'll make sure you have help," Matthew said. "I'm not going to leave you high and dry. I'm giving you a good way to start making the ranch profitable."

"Aren't you worried I'll run it into the ground again?"

"Dad," Matthew started. He looked to Parker and she could see that he wished she could respond for him, but she didn't have the answers. "We'll figure something out. But you have to have the surgery. The appointment the other day, the surgeon said you have to get on the list because it could be a couple of months before you get in for surgery."

"Fine, I'll call him." Buck leaned back on the bed. "Are they letting me out of here tonight?"

Parker handed Faith over to Matthew. "Let me go check and see what they're planning for you, Buck."

"I was going to fix you a nice dinner tonight."

"Maybe I'll cook dinner for you," she offered.

"Now that sounds mighty nice," Buck said. "But I already have it planned."

Parker left to find the doctor to discuss Buck's care and his discharge. A conversation with Dr. Adams helped her feel in control again. It helped her to concentrate on something other than the man in that room and the baby he held.

Her life had taken so many twists and turns lately, she was starting to think she needed a road map to get back on track. She could almost hear her dad telling her that she had a road map, but it wouldn't do her any good at all if she never opened it.

"She's a good girl," Parker heard Buck saying as she returned to the room. She hesitated, not wanting to interrupt, not wanting to listen to something not meant for her. She started to turn and go back to the nurse's station.

"I know she is, Dad. She's one of the best people I know."

"Then why don't you ask her out?"

Silence.

"Because she was my best friend and I'm not sure I can give her more."

She closed her eyes, wishing for all the world she hadn't heard. At that point, walking away was pointless. She opened the door and entered, catching them both with guilty expressions.

"Dr. Adams is going to run a few more tests. He'll have you out of here this afternoon. I hope you brought bottles for Faith. If you didn't, we can get extras from the nursery."

"I have bottles and formula, a dozen diapers." The dimpled look he gave her disarmed her completely and she almost forgot the conversation between him and his father.

The conversation where, once again, she was the best friend.

Chapter Eleven

Matthew pulled up to the rambling, two-story farmhouse that had been in his family for nearly a century. There were five bedrooms, two bathrooms—added after indoor plumbing became available—and a kitchen that would make a chef envious. Matthew guessed his mother's family money had remodeled the kitchen. Izzy Rivers was a Bowen from Tulsa. In her world, that meant something. The kitchen had been her imprint on the house. She'd given them life and a kitchen and then she'd left.

Yeah, so maybe he was still holding on to some bitterness. Lately he'd been thinking about that, about the things he'd held on to. And the things he'd let go. All of it seemed to be festering, forcing him to deal with the past. Forgive. That seemed to be the theme of his troubled conscience. Forgive his parents. Forgive himself.

Forgive God? Nah, that wasn't the thing a man had to do. He had to let go, though, and accept. One of the stages of grief: acceptance. It felt a lot better than the denial and the anger.

Matthew parked in front of the house. He sat for a

minute, staring at the place he'd resented as a kid and realizing the resentment seemed to be fading. He shifted to look at Buck. Grizzled and gray, but sharp. Buck had always seemed old, but he really wasn't. He was just broken like the rest of them. Somewhere, Matthew had learned that it wasn't too late.

"Buck," Matthew started, catching his father's attention. Buck frowned. "Dad," Matthew corrected. "I need to say something."

"You sending me to one of them old folks' homes?" Buck said with a grin.

"I don't think they call them that."

"I reckon they don't."

"I'm sorry for not being around more." Matthew had planned on telling Buck he was forgiven, but then realized he needed to make his own amends. "I let anger control my life. I realize now that I need to forgive you, and Izzy."

Step one to a new life. Maybe in time he'd be ready to return to Chicago and his ministry. He guessed maybe part of coming home had been for this, for putting this life to rights.

"I guess forgiven just took on a whole new meaning," Buck said as he closed his eyes. "Thank you, son."

Matthew nodded, not sure what to say or how to say it. "We should go in. Parker just pulled up. She'll help get you comfortable."

"I'm comfortable. That shot did a world of good. I feel like I could go work some cows, maybe even ride a horse."

"Get this surgery and you'll be doing those things."

"Right, the surgery." Buck sighed. "Maybe if I put it off, you'll stick around a little longer."

Matthew shook his head and pushed his door open. As he rounded the truck to help Buck, he made eye contact with Parker. She was on the phone as she unhooked Faith from her car seat.

Buck had taken it upon himself to get out of the truck. He had the cane in his left hand and he bent his knee a bit, probably checking to see how the shot had worked.

"Feeling good. I'm almost a spring chicken. I'll head on in and you tend to the ladies." Buck, cane in hand, headed for the front door.

Matthew turned to "the ladies." Parker had the handle of the seat in her hand, the diaper bag thrown over her shoulder. She'd ended her call, but from the look on her face, the call had ended her. She blinked fast and angled her head so he couldn't see her expression.

"What happened?" he asked as he reached to take the carrier. She shook her head, not letting go. "Parker?"

She closed her eyes, her expression somewhere between serene and brokenhearted. In the late afternoon sun, the light touched her hair, touched her cheeks and all of it touched him. He had spent thirty-six years being a bachelor and not once had he ever felt the way he did at that moment, as if the person in front of him meant more than himself. The power of that thought scared the daylights out of him. He wanted to protect her, to set her world to rights, to give her the moon if possible.

But deep down, he didn't know if he could ever be good enough for her. The silence that held them grew as she struggled to fight tears. He knew something definitely needed to be said. He just didn't know what. For that reason, he pulled her close and held her.

"They found a potential home. For Faith." She added the last as if he might not know.

"Oh," he said, the word dropping between them. He hadn't expected it to feel like loss. "How? I mean, who?"

"A couple in Tulsa. They're expecting, but they think they could handle Faith. They want to try."

"So a temporary home," he said.

"Hopefully not," she said and then she rested her head against his shoulder. "We should go in."

They started for the house.

"I knew it would hurt, but this is worse than hurt."

"I know." He led her up the front steps of the house. "It's okay to feel hurt."

Her expression changed and he knew those had definitely been the wrong words to say.

"But I'm cheerful, happy Parker, always optimistic, always believing the best in every situation."

"You don't have to be that person for me. That isn't how friendship works. With a friend, you can be yourself, whatever version of yourself you need to be. If you need to fall apart, then I'm here, because I'm your friend."

"I don't need to fall apart," she said after a minute. "Thank you, for being the friend who would let me be that person." She pinched the bridge of her nose, shaking her head. And then she cried.

He held her tight as the tears fell, and the sobs shook her body. He leaned a cheek against the top of her head, trying to absorb her heartache. It was his heartache, too. Faith had become precious to him. Parker, too.

"I feel so ridiculous." She spoke with her face still buried in his shoulder.

"You're not ridiculous."

She glanced up at him with watery eyes and parted lips. He realized then that he was no longer holding her to comfort her. He was holding her because he wanted her in his arms.

The invitation of her parted lips proved to be more than he could resist. He leaned, touched his lips to hers and tasted her cherry lip gloss and the saltiness of her tears. He held her in his arms as the kiss grew deeper and changed to something that not only took, but gave. Her free arm wrapped around his neck and he felt her fingers move through his hair.

In the quiet recesses of his mind, a memory stabbed at his conscience—the memory of her voice, young and embarrassed as she told him she loved him.

"Parker," he whispered as he pulled away.

"Don't," she said. "Please don't say anything about friendship or mistakes. I don't want to be your mistake. I'm sick of always being the best friend."

"That wasn't about friendship," he assured her.

Fortunately, or maybe unfortunately, Faith let out a squeak, reminding them of her presence.

"She's probably starting to get hungry. I should take her to the camper."

Which meant they weren't discussing this, not anytime soon.

The door opened. Pete the dog ran out. Buck appeared, looking sheepish. "You two coming inside?"

Pete ran circles around them, his tail wagging, thumping against their legs, against the infant carrier that was now empty, because Parker had pulled the baby out and held her close.

"Pete, down." Matthew snapped his fingers and

pointed. The black-and-white dog came to a sliding halt, trembling with excitement. "Yes, we're coming in."

"Good thing. I forgot that I put a roast in the Crock-Pot this morning. It's ready to eat, if you're ready?"

"I should go…" Parker started.

Buck waved his arm a bit. "Now don't start that. I've got a roast with potatoes and carrots and some of those rolls you heat and eat. You might as well join us."

She looked at Matthew, waiting. He knew where her hesitancy came from. Buck had probably been peeking out the windows and also knew what had happened on the front porch.

"Come inside. You need to be with family and for now, that's what we are."

She gave him a quick, teary nod.

They entered the house together. The curtains were drawn, and the interior remained in shadows made by a dimly lit lamp in one corner of the exhausted, aging living room with its furnishings a tribute to the 1980s.

Buck said something about needing to change over a load of laundry and he hobbled away without looking back. Matthew guessed that was his father's version of giving them time and allowing Parker to gather up her emotions. Buck had never been a fan of emotional scenes. The night Izzy left, he'd also left. Neither of the parents had thought about how their desertion had affected their children.

The cat appeared, pretending for the moment to be an ally. The orange feline rubbed against Matthew's legs.

"The cat, as you know, is a villain who pretends to be your friend and then attacks when you're least expecting it."

She laughed and he loved the sound and the way

it chased away the storm cloud expression she'd been wearing. As they walked from living room to dining room and then to the kitchen, she appeared to be taking it all in: this sad excuse for a home.

As they entered the kitchen, the very modern kitchen that stood as a stark contrast to the rest of the house, she hesitated, looking surprised.

"My mother's one contribution. She loved to cook and this was her domain."

Buck had returned and he gave Matthew a sharp look.

"She gave more than just this kitchen," Buck said, his voice raspy. "She gave me five children."

"That she did."

Buck pointed to pictures on the walls. "I have you all right here."

Matthew had studied the framed photographs of himself and his siblings, surprised by the sentimental nature of the images captured and framed. There was even a framed article about Matthew and Jared, the church they'd started in a home that had moved to more homes, then a gymnasium and finally a building of their own. He'd lived in an apartment on the church campus because it hadn't seemed necessary to rent a place for just himself. The church had bought Jared a parsonage.

"I visited," Parker said as she handed him Faith, helping him to cradle the infant with her head supported. "I need to make her a bottle."

He took the baby, holding her close and speaking in a voice that she seemed to enjoy, but the words were for Parker.

"You visited?"

"Yes, your church. I visited when I was working in the Chicago area."

"You never said anything."

He pictured her at the back of the auditorium, the way she'd been as a teenager, taking notes for one of her father's sermons. She'd been there and he hadn't known. "You didn't talk to me."

"And relive my great embarrassment? I don't think so."

He wished she had spoken to him, contacted him. He understood why she hadn't. He wanted to tell her again how sorry he was for what he'd done. It was the wrong time for the words, but the right time to put it behind them.

She moved around the kitchen, making the bottle, ignoring him. The cat followed her, not showing the slightest signs of attack.

"How is Miss Philips?" she asked.

"I visited her the other day. She's hoping she can come home soon. I'm also hopeful, too. That cat needs her."

The cat pounced on his foot.

"Sam's adorable," Parker said, amusement twinkling in her eyes.

Matthew studied the pair, woman and cat. "I can think of a lot of adjectives for that cat. Adorable isn't one."

She handed him a bottle and the look they shared caused him to lose his breath. She was beautiful, the type of beauty that was heart-and-soul deep, with eyes that mirrored her faith and her love for people. He'd never thought about how this would feel, to want a woman to look at him that way.

She was the eighth wonder of the world, and she didn't even know it. If he told her, she wouldn't believe him. He had a sneaking suspicion that she would think he was trying to make up for the past. Silence seemed the best course of action. For the time being.

He'd loved her as a friend. He knew enough about life to realize he might be falling in love with the woman she'd become.

"You feed Faith and I'll help Buck set the table," Parker said as she headed back to the safety of the kitchen. Safe because it put distance between her and the man who had looked at her the way she used to dream about him looking at her.

It was just the day, the baby, all of the memories. That had to be the reason for the tension in the air and the look on his face. She wasn't about to let herself fall for a man who had always kept her in the category of friend. After having heard it just that day, she knew exactly where she stood.

She didn't want to think about Matthew. She also didn't want to think about the phone call with Jackie. It might be true that Parker would be leaving in a matter of weeks. That didn't mean she wanted to hand Faith over to another family. Her heart would break.

It was already breaking.

Somehow, she needed to keep things in perspective. This was and had always been about what would be best for Faith. A family with two parents, siblings and all of the other things a child deserved.

"Buck, how'd you become a cook?" Parker asked, ready for a diversion.

Buck winked at her as he handed her a bowl of potatoes. She'd never noticed before, but father and son were carbon copies of one another.

"I've spent a lot of years alone and I needed a hobby, especially since I quit drinking. When I'm tempted by the bottle, I watch one of those cooking shows and make something new. Of course, a roast isn't new, but it's always one of my favorites."

They sat down together at the maple wood kitchen table, a fresh vase of flowers in the center. It all seemed strangely at odds. Buck, the house, the meal and the run-down farm, plus the fact that she was there, sitting between the two of them. Matthew still held Faith. She rested on his shoulder and he managed to eat with one hand holding the baby.

"Roast might not be new, but this is the best roast I've ever had," Parker said as they finished the meal.

"Thank you, it's my own special recipe."

"I didn't even know that I liked roast," Matthew told his father.

"Well, I doubt I ever cooked it for you when you were growing up." Buck looked a little embarrassed. "I don't know that we had a meal together after Izzy left."

"Only the ones we ate at Chuck's." Matthew shifted Faith and cradled her in his arm. "Or frozen dinners we heated in the microwave. We ate a lot of potpies."

"I'm sorry about that," Buck said and then he grinned. "Did you know my son is planning on preaching at the community church?"

That was one way to change the subject.

"Thanks, Dad."

Matthew pushed back from the table and he handed

Faith over. The tender look on his face melted her heart. The next look, the warning one he gave Buck, that look didn't have the same effect.

Matthew started clearing the table. When she moved to help, he shook his head. "You worked all day. Take a few minutes and rest."

"Thank you," she told him as she cuddled the infant. "I should put her down while she is sleeping. I'm learning to sleep when I can, and that means sleeping when she sleeps."

The mention of sleep made her suddenly tired. She covered a yawn with her free hand. Matthew gave her a quick look.

"You work tomorrow?"

She shook her head. "I'm off. Fortunately. Jackie wants to meet at Wagoner, so we can let this family meet Faith."

"I'll go with you," he offered.

"You don't have to."

"I want to, so don't argue."

Buck cleared his throat as he moved from his seat. "I should probably tend to my chickens. I'll have a dozen eggs for you tomorrow. I'll have Matthew bring them down to you."

Buck patted her shoulder, the gesture awkward but sweet.

"You're a real treasure. Someone is going to be very blessed to have you as a wife."

She didn't have words for that comment. "Buck, you're the treasure. I enjoyed this meal, and the company."

"You're welcome anytime," Buck said. "And I'd

rather the two of you leave the dishes. On nights that I can't sleep, I clean my kitchen. I'll finish them up later."

Buck went out the back door. They could hear him shuffling around, hear him talking to the cat and the dog. Parker smiled at the sounds.

"I'll walk you back to the camper," Matthew told her as he put the last plate in the dishwasher. "If I don't leave something for Buck to wash, he'll probably be in here cooking another meal."

"I can walk myself back to the camper."

"I want to go with you. You carry Faith, I'll grab the seat and her bag."

They left the house, side by side. It was a beautiful spring night. The sun was setting in the west, turning the sky pink and lavender. The trees were dark against the brilliant colors. In the distance, a fox yipped and others replied. Sounds of the country. The air smelled different here, of freshly mowed grass and wildflowers, no exhaust, no pollution. She didn't mind working in larger cities, but the country called to her. It was a part of her.

"Are you really going to preach on Sunday?"

He shrugged, looking thoughtful, maybe a little distracted.

"I don't know. I'm not sure why they want me to speak. I'm not sure if I'm ready. What if I get up there and say something like, 'God doesn't answer prayers'?"

"Maybe you could say that God doesn't always give us the answer we prayed for, the miracle we expected. Maybe you could tell them that when life is difficult, God is still with us? He is God, He can handle our very human emotions."

"What if…?" he started.

"So many of those in life," she teased.

His eyes crinkled at the corners. "Yes, so many what ifs. I'll think about preaching."

"I'll come and listen. I'll even say hello afterwards."

"I'm counting on you being there. I don't think I can do this alone."

She slipped her hand in his. "You won't be alone. Even if I'm not there, you know that He is there."

"Are you trusting Him in this situation with Faith?" he asked as they reached the porch of the camper.

"Yes. As hard as this is, I'm trusting Him. As much as I want to solve the problem and make things happen in the way I want, I'm trusting that His plan is best. It might hurt, but I've been hurt before."

She yawned again. Matthew opened the camper door, left the seat and diaper bag and walked back out to where she'd taken a seat on the lounge chair next to a fire pit.

"Go to sleep," he ordered as he leaned over and dropped a kiss on her cheek. He then took Faith from her arms. "I'll change her diaper and fix her a bottle. We'll be fine out here while you get some rest."

"I can take care of her." Parker rubbed at her eyes to give herself a jolt and wake up. "This day has been a lot."

"Yes, it has. The past few weeks have been a lot. Take a nap, Parker."

"You can come inside," she told him.

He dimpled at the invitation. "Nah, I think I'll sit out here for a bit. It's warm. I can use the air, and I think

Faith enjoys being outside. Also, I'm afraid if I come in there, I'm going to want to kiss you again."

A tear trickled down her cheek. She brushed it away. She wasn't this person, the one who cried at the drop of a hat.

"It was a kiss, Matthew. I'm not going to say it wasn't a nice kiss—it was, but it won't happen again. It can't. We're both adults and we know how this ends."

"How does it end?" He seemed truly curious.

"With one or both of us leaving Sunset Ridge. It ends with you staying on here, or maybe you won't—I don't know the exact details—but I do know that it ends. When it does, it'll hurt."

She closed her eyes at the admission. She really was tired.

"I don't want to hurt you," he said.

"We'll always be friends." She repeated one of the things he'd said in the now infamous phone call, ashamed that she wanted to hurt him with the words. "I'll be fine with Faith."

She took the baby, wishing she hadn't gone down this path, hadn't said the words she'd said. She was so tired, she didn't know how to take it back or how to fix things.

As soon as she was inside and the door closed behind her, she sank to the floor. The dog had followed her inside. As she sat with Faith held close and tears trickling down her cheeks, the pet crawled close to place his head on her lap.

"*I'll never love you, Parker, not that way. You're my best friend.*" That's how he'd ended the fateful phone call years ago.

It seemed they were still good friends. But the teen Matthew hadn't kissed her the way he kissed her tonight. He hadn't looked at her the way a man who loves a woman might look at her, as if she was the most important person in his life. If she hadn't heard what he'd said to his dad, she might have believed that look.

Chapter Twelve

"Why are we doing this?" Matthew asked as they walked up to the county office the day after she'd shut him out of her life and the camper.

He didn't know what he meant by the question and from the puzzled look on her face, neither did she. Did he mean why were they circling each other like Sam and Pete, or did he mean the meeting with the prospective foster parents?

"We're doing this because it's the right thing to do," she eventually answered. They were on the sidewalk just feet away from the entrance. "We're doing this because I'm leaving in June. I have a contract to finish and a job in Destin."

"Do you have to pay to get out of this contract?"

"No, of course not."

"Could you stay here?" he asked.

She shook her head a little too aggressively and he guessed she could stay if she wanted. He also guessed that she wouldn't stay. Because of him? What if he left? Would she stay? He should have asked, but she didn't give him a chance. She had the door open and motioned him through with Faith.

"Next week I start my temporary position as chaplain," he said in an offhanded way, just trying to get her attention. He'd decided to take the job because he couldn't refuse to help Chaplain Rogers, not when he desperately needed the time off.

"You'll make an excellent chaplain." Her gaze remained averted. "I'm also looking forward to church on Sunday."

"You and dozens of other curious onlookers. It's like I'm the accident on the side of the road that everyone wants to witness."

"They want to hear you because you are gifted."

The compliment called for humility. "Thank you, Parker. And could we call a truce? I don't think this tension is good for Faith. Or for us."

"You're right. I'm sorry." Her steps faltered, as if she'd just realized what would happen in the next few minutes. "I know this is the right thing to do."

"I'm trusting you on this," he said. "Because I really don't know. I look at this baby girl and I can't imagine life without her. That sounds crazy because she shouldn't even be in our lives. She's here by chance and, I guess, so are we."

"Is it by chance?"

"We could turn and leave. We could call Jackie and tell her we've changed our mind."

"She isn't ours to keep, Matthew. She doesn't belong to us. Not that we are an 'us.'"

"We could be." The proposal slipped out and he could feel the color drain from his face, watched the color drain from hers as the meaning behind his words sank in.

"Stop being ridiculous," she said it as if she wanted to pretend he'd been joking.

He wasn't even sure how he meant for her to take what he'd said. He'd been thinking of solutions, for Faith and for Parker, a way to keep them safe, to keep Parker smiling the way she smiled when Faith slept in her arms.

He'd thought about himself and how it would feel when this ended and they were no longer together, no longer parenting Faith. They'd never planned for this to be permanent. They'd gone into this caregiving situation knowing it would be temporary. Just as he'd come back home, telling himself it was temporary. The proposal, if that's what it had been, had slipped out and now he didn't know how to feel about her reaction. Ridiculous. Maybe it was.

Maybe not. He was slowly stepping back up to responsibilities—the chaplain job, the upcoming sermon. Why not continue? It seemed part of a natural progression. Perhaps this was the way they were meant to be. "I'm not ridiculous. We could get married and give her a home."

"And now I know you've lost your mind," she said as her brown eyes turned liquid. "You said it yourself—we're friends and that's all we could ever be."

"A good marriage is based on friendship."

"Nope. I'm not playing this game of 'what if' with you. I'm not the person you would ever fall in love with. There are probably many reasons for that, but let's start with how I'm almost thirty-five, which is knocking on the door of middle-aged."

"I'm thirty-six."

"And you're..." She shook her head. "Oh, stop. Please,

just stop. You're making a difficult day even more difficult."

"I meant to make it easier." It slammed him like a thunderbolt. He did want to marry her. The reasons went beyond giving Faith a home. He wanted the best for Parker. He wanted her to be happy. He couldn't imagine a day without her in his life. That was the part that nearly undid his composure as tears leaked from her brown eyes. He'd messed up. He should have done this differently and at a different time.

"There isn't a way to make this easy." Her words were softly spoken and had a ring of finality.

A door at the end of the hall opened. Jackie stepped out, paused, gave them both a strong look. "Everything okay out here?"

"Perfect," Parker said with a bright look, as if she might mean it. "We're coming."

"Good. The Jansens are waiting." Jackie motioned them forward, a hesitant smile on as she looked from one to the other of them. "Parker, it isn't too late."

Parker shook her head. "We're doing the right thing."

"It doesn't feel right," Matthew mumbled as they entered the office.

The Jansens were a nice couple, early-thirties. He worked in banking. She sold real estate but had taken time off to raise a family. They wanted a big family, starting with the baby they would have in five months.

"In five months, Faith will be six months old." Parker made that statement. "You'll have a newborn and a six-month-old."

"I think we can do it," Vicky Jansen said with a warm look as her hand went to her belly. "I've had some terrible morning sickness. That's the only reason we've hesitated to foster. We went through the training, got licensed, then found out we were having a baby of our own. It's all been a lot and we needed to take time to think about the situation. When Jackie called about Faith, we just weren't sure."

"We're still wanting a little time to think on this," Daron Jansen said, smiling at his wife as he did. "We wanted to meet you all and meet Faith. We don't want to make a decision that would be harmful to her, or to us, to the baby we're having."

Matthew held Parker's gaze for an instant before she handed the baby over to Vicky Jansen. He wanted to say something, anything that would stop this from happening. The warning look Parker gave him stopped him from speaking.

He pulled back, letting her take the lead. Maybe she was right. Maybe he'd reacted to the situation. He'd acted impulsively, wanting to fix things for her. The best thing he could do for them was give it time and think about what had motivated him to propose.

"She's beautiful," Vicky Jansen said as she cooed at the baby in her arms. "Absolutely precious. Any idea yet about the mother or any other family?"

"None," Jackie said. "At this point, we're moving toward permanency for her. A family that will adopt."

"What if mom shows back up, or some other family member?"

Jackie looked as if they'd just backed her into a corner, but she quickly returned to her composed self, sure and determined. "There is always that chance. We won't move so quickly that a biological family member doesn't have the opportunity to come forward. There will be hearings, notices in local papers and obviously the police are still searching for the mother."

"She's a precious little girl," Daron Jansen said. He reached for Faith's fingers, touched them gently.

Matthew guessed that Daron Jansen was a man who knew how to be a father. From the look he gave his wife, he also knew how to be a husband. Matthew had spent a lifetime convincing himself he would never step into either arena and therefore he wouldn't have to worry about a broken family. Or a broken heart.

As he looked from that baby to Parker, he realized how wrong he'd been about the broken heart.

Parker wanted to escape the room, the meeting, the emotions that were like a storm crashing against her heart. As she sat there watching the Jansens with Faith, she wanted to scream that it wasn't fair. She would never be a mother. She would never have a husband who held her so sweetly, as if she was the most precious person in his life.

All of her life she'd been taught that envy was a sin, and yet, there she sat, filled with envy. It threatened to engulf her as she watched the other woman hold the baby she'd cared for all these weeks. Vicky Jansen's hand went to her rounded belly, where another baby grew. A baby that would be loved and nurtured by parents who adored her.

She wanted to be the person that a man longed to have in his life. She wanted to know that when he proposed, he meant it because he couldn't live his life without her. No matter how noble Matthew's proposal had been, it hadn't been spurred by that kind of love. It had been spurred by friendship and duty and that hurt worse than being told they could only ever be friends.

He didn't want to marry her, he wanted to save Faith. As much as she wanted Faith, she wouldn't accept a marriage that wasn't real and honest in God's eyes.

She stood, not really thinking about what she planned to do or where she planned to go. The others in the room turned to look at her.

"I'm going to get a drink." She said the first thing to come to her mind.

"There's a kitchen down the hall and bottled water in the fridge," Jackie offered.

With a nod, she left the room and closed the door behind her because if they said anything sympathetic, she might cry. She made it to the kitchen before the tears started to fall. Burying her face in her hands, she leaned against the wall, needing support to keep from sinking to the ground.

Strong arms circled her. She knew his scent, knew his touch. His lips brushed the top of her head and she cried all the harder for his kindness during this impossible time.

She should push him away because his arms around her only made this all more confusing.

"I'm sorry." He held her close as he said the words.

"I hate this," she said on a strangled cry. "I don't want that family to take her."

"I know." He gently rocked her as he held her. "I want her to have you. Only you."

Not the two of them. He'd taken back the proposal. Already. But of course he had, because he'd had a few minutes to think it through and he knew how wrong it had been. She'd known it from the moment the words had been spoken that they'd been impulsive and he'd come to regret them. She didn't know whether to walk away or lean into him. She needed his comfort, but she felt anger rise up at his glib offer that they could be a family. Perhaps to him it had been a solution to a problem. For her it was a cruel reminder of what she'd longed for all of those years ago.

She forced herself to move out of his arms because she couldn't rely on him for comfort or strength. She pulled a few napkins from a holder on a nearby table and wiped her eyes, knowing she would look a mess after crying. She didn't care. Her swollen eyes and red nose were nothing compared to how her heart crumbled, feeling as if it might never be whole again.

"Parker, I'm sorry."

"You don't need to apologize," she said, managing to sound strong. "I know that she'll be better with them. They can give her a home, a family and a yard with a dog."

"You can give her love."

"Yes, I can." She drew in a shaky breath and maintained her distance from him. "I can, but that doesn't make it right. My wanting her doesn't make me the best person for her."

The same way his proposal didn't make them a couple. It didn't mean anything to him, other than a way for her to keep Faith. And as angry and hurt as she felt, a small part of her wanted to accept. For Faith.

"Doesn't it?" he questioned, drawing her back to the conversation.

"Stop," she warned. "I know you're trying to point out that I could do this. Or we could do this. I'm trying to be realistic."

"I know you are."

Footsteps in the hall finished their conversation. Jackie stepped into the kitchen, concern in her hazel eyes.

"You both okay?" she asked.

"We're working on that," Matthew told the caseworker. Parker shot him a look, begging him to not say anything, to not do something that might jeopardize this home for Faith.

"Good," Jackie said. "I know this isn't easy for either of you. You've been her primary caregivers, her support while she was hospitalized. You have a bond, and she is better for that bond. Don't worry, I'm not here to talk you into something that isn't right for you. The Jansens are wonderful and they seem very taken with her. They're thinking in the next few weeks, they could transition her to their home. Maybe start with having her a day or two next weekend, then a few days the week after. They want her to be able to bond with them, but not so drastically that it upsets her world overly much."

"I think that is the best idea," Parker said. She looked to Matthew, needing him to agree.

"Yes, sounds good to me."

She knew from his expression that it didn't sound good to him. What choice did they have?

"Okay, then this is the way it will play out." Jackie looked less convinced than before. "We'll meet here next Thursday and the Jansens will take Faith for a night, possibly two if she seems content. Can one of you bring Faith, her seat, her bassinet, bottles and whatever else she might need?"

Parker closed her eyes and nodded. "I can bring her."

"I'll come with you," Matthew offered.

She shook her head. “I’d like to do this alone. If you don’t mind.”

He studied her face so intently that she feared he knew her thoughts. She couldn’t do this with him. They’d been sharing responsibilities. He’d watched Faith while she worked. They both loved the little girl. She needed separation from him. She needed to be able to say good-bye to Faith and she needed to be able to walk away from both Faith and Matthew. Without the baby, she didn’t have the man.

“If you change your mind, I can go to the hospital afterwards.”

He would be filling the role of chaplain that day. She might need him after dropping Faith with people who were basically strangers to her.

Fifteen minutes later, they left. Parker managed to smile at the couple who would be taking Faith. She managed to shake their hands, avoiding the hugs that would cause her to lose control of her emotions. They were good people. She didn’t doubt their goodness. She didn’t dislike them.

She envied them. As the thought poked at her, she knew it was wrong. Envy meant to want what someone else had rather than acknowledging how blessed she was. She knew she was blessed. She had to focus on the good in her life. She had to pray and know that God had this situation in His hand and He knew the very best plan for their lives.

Parker left the building with Faith in her arms. The baby woke up and seemed to smile up at her with a little baby grin. Matthew’s arms stole around her waist and she didn’t pull away, not this time. She needed the comfort of his touch, even if it was temporary.

Chapter Thirteen

Sunday morning sunshine glistened off fields damp from the overnight rain. Matthew breathed deeply of the fresh air, perfumed with the country scents of soil, wildflowers and pure Oklahoma. In the distance, he heard… silence. The silence of the country. And then, singing.

Parker.

He paused on his walk to the barn and listened. His lips tugged upward, a response to that sound and the way it did something to his heart, a heart that he'd have told anyone was encased in concrete. Until Parker.

The last few weeks in her presence had changed things. She'd unknowingly chipped away at the walls surrounding his heart.

He'd always cared about people. He wasn't so callous that he didn't want the best for people in his life. But with Parker, it was different. So different it shifted the whole trajectory of his life.

He hadn't realized just how much she'd changed things for him until they'd stood together at the family services office and he'd realized marrying her would fix everything. Maybe even his heart. It had been impulsive and she sure hadn't taken it well, and afterwards he'd realized how crazy it must have seemed to her.

In the days since, he'd given the proposal a lot of thought, trying to make sense of it. Had it been duty driven? The same kind of duty that caused him to take over the hospital chaplaincy, had him helping his father and also checking on Miss Phillips while caring for her cat?

Or had the proposal been spurred by deeper feelings that he needed time to figure out?

He hadn't counted on Parker being so dead set on finding her path and protecting herself from being hurt. He'd just been trying to follow the arrow. The arrow that went straight to Parker.

He reached the barn and stopped at the corner, listening like a little boy trying to learn secrets not meant for him. She was singing a hymn about standing on the promises. No one stood the way she stood. She was a rock. Even now, with everything in turmoil, she was standing on the promises.

He went back to his chores, because she deserved her privacy and he needed some of his own. Today he would go before the small congregation of Sunset Ridge Community Church and preach a message that promised to be difficult. It promised to hurt. The pain, most of it, would be his. This was his day of reckoning.

He needed to know that his words were the right words and that his heart followed those words.

A whinny from the corral caught his attention. He shifted directions and walked around the corner of the barn. The mare and foal were there, golden and glistening in the sunshine. The mare tossed her pretty head, shaking her flaxen mane.

"Good morning, pretty girl." He leaned against the top board of the corral, now stable from all the repairs he and Buck had done. "Ready for breakfast?"

The mare trotted up to the fence. She nuzzled his hand and he gave her a good petting on her neck, the kind that caused her to lean in and then turn and nip at his sleeve when he stopped.

"I'd love to hang out with you all day, but I have somewhere to go." He stood for a minute, trying to coax her little filly to the fence. "Come on, princess."

The filly took a few hesitant steps and nuzzled his fingers before backing away. Something in the grass caught her attention. She leaned, her neck still not matching up to her long legs. A toad hopped away and the filly took off, prancing and kicking up her back legs. The mare left to tend to her offspring.

Matthew did his chores and went back to the house. Buck was up, but moving slower today than in days past.

Today Matthew planned on calling his brothers and his sister. They should all know what was going on with Buck—the surgery, his sobriety, all of it. He couldn't make them forgive, but he could encourage it. Jael and Luke, being the two who lived closest, should at least try and visit more often.

Mark… Well, Mark had a whole lot of baggage to work through. Matthew thought the first steps for Mark would be a program to get clean and then making amends with his wife and daughter. Again, no one could make him. Matthew just prayed that rock bottom wouldn't land him in jail or worse.

Jonah, poor Jonah, had been the baby until Jael came along. He'd been about four when Izzy left. That meant

his care had fallen to his older brothers. They hadn't been too loving or too gentle with him.

No wonder they were all such a mess. Each one of them single and afraid to take a chance on a long-term relationship. Statistically, children of divorce were more likely to divorce. Knowing how much that had hurt, Matthew had avoided the institution of marriage for fear of having kids who would suffer the way he and his siblings had suffered.

"Ready to go?" Buck walked into the kitchen where Matthew was pouring himself a cup of coffee to take with him.

"Yeah, just about. I got you a present."

Buck leaned on the counter as he grabbed a cup out of the cabinet. "What's that?"

Matthew pushed the walker across the floor. The doctor had recommended one. Buck was stubborn.

"This. Use it."

His dad blustered while pouring coffee. "I ain't going to use no walker like I'm an old man who can't walk on his own two feet."

"No, you're not, but you're in pain and the doctor said with both knees a mess, this would help. It'll save you energy and you can do more."

Buck grumbled under his breath, something about Matthew being a lot of trouble.

Matthew chuckled as he put a lid on his coffee cup. "Come on, Dad. Let's get to church. I want to get this over with."

"Shouldn't you be happy to share the Lord's word?"

"I'm not sure how I feel about it."

They walked out the front door. Pete was there, sprawled out on the porch. Parker sat on the old porch swing with Faith strapped in the seat and ready to go.

"Good morning," she called out as she put her feet down to stop the swing.

Matthew hesitated, his cup to his lips. He'd thought the morning was beautiful, sunny and green, a hint of humidity and warmth in the air. It didn't hold a candle to Parker with her hair shimmering around her shoulders and a summery coral shade on her lips. She wore a dress that matched her lipstick.

An elbow hit him in the ribs. "Say something," Buck whispered.

"Ready for church?" he asked.

She'd stood and joined them while he'd been speechless. She looked nearly perfect, standing there holding Faith. He thought back to his impulsive proposal that had seemed to be driven by his sense of duty and he knew, more than ever, that it had been driven by what he felt for her.

He cleared his throat.

"I am. Are you?" She smiled as she answered. They were on decent footing again. She seemed to have forgiven the proposal and probably thought it best to go on as if it hadn't happened.

"As ready as I'll ever be." He took the infant seat from her. Faith seemed to smile a little.

"It's church," Buck reminded him. "You're not walking the plank."

Right.

Forty-five minutes later, he stood before the congregation of the church Parker's father once pastored and let his gaze roam over the packed pews. The dying little church was overflowing. Because of him? If so, they were going to be disappointed.

"I want to thank you all for joining us today. This sermon might be a little different than you expected, but I hope it will be honest and maybe we will take something from this."

He swept his gaze over the congregation. "I'm not even sure if I'm called to preach. I'm angry at God. I'm not sure if my prayers matter. I…" He felt the warmth of peace as he stood there searching for words that made sense. He realized he'd always felt that peace when he stood before a congregation. He'd been fighting against peace.

He'd been fighting guilt. He realized it as sure as he breathed. He'd felt guilty for living.

"I'm here because I had to find my way back to the person God called me to be. I had to trust Him and allow Him to direct my paths. Because, you see, the path He sets us on is a blessed path. It might not always be easy, but the end result is a blessing. The path you create for yourself will take you on a journey, but it might not be a peaceful journey."

He caught Parker's gaze and held it. He needed to have someone to focus on. She was his anchor, his harbor in a storm, and she had no idea.

"I spent a big portion of my life being angry and resenting my father. I'm sorry, Dad." He shifted to look at Buck. "And in the past weeks, I've come to realize that my bitterness hadn't hurt Buck—not in the way I expected. My bitterness and unforgiveness were a cancer in my life and they hurt everyone around me. People who mattered to me. Forgiving my father wasn't something I needed to do for him, not really. It was for me, so I could let go of old wounds and let them heal. We're called to forgive. We're called to keep loving one another earnestly because love covers a multitude of sins. I've been on a journey recently and fortunately, God has been on this journey with me."

He went on, sharing verses on forgiveness and encouraging people to let go of anger that takes control, growing until it robs a person of the fruit of God's Spirit. The message wasn't long, but he'd never been one to preach too long if he felt he'd delivered the message he was called on to give.

At the close, he invited anyone in need of prayer to come to the altar. As he stepped down off the stage, Buck was there.

"I need more of Jesus," Buck said as he took Matthew's hand. "And I need to tell you again how sorry I am."

"Me, too, Dad." Matthew put an arm around his father and they prayed.

The words would bring healing. Acting on them would take them further. It wouldn't happen in a day and it might be a continuing process, but it was a beginning.

He caught sight of Parker. She was kneeling at the altar and he moved to kneel next to her. She reached for his hand, but she didn't share her need. He didn't push.

Instead he prayed silently for his own needs. The prayer took him by surprise, because it wasn't the prayer he would have imagined. He also knew, deep down, that if he told her what was on his heart, she'd pull away from him.

First, she had to trust him. And, he guessed, she also needed time to forgive him. He didn't know if she could do either, not enough to let him into her life the way he thought God planned.

As Parker pushed to her feet, she looked up at the cowboy preacher who'd once been her best friend. He didn't wear his hat, but she could see the indention where it normally sat. She met his silvery gray eyes and she wished she didn't feel so much when she looked at him.

"I forgive you," she said out loud and she let the words wash over her. "We're friends again, but I've resented you for a very long time. I made it a habit, blaming you for my sadness, blaming you for my brokenness. That's over. I forgive you."

"I'm so sorry I hurt you," he told her and he meant it—she could see it in his eyes. He hadn't known, but now he did and he was sorry. "Maybe we were both brought back here at this time for this purpose, to forgive and to heal."

"Maybe." Now that the words were said, she wanted to escape.

Fortunately for her, people were moving forward to thank him for his open and honest sermon and for the message. She heard one of the members ask if he might consider preaching again sometime. He said he'd consider it.

Lean not unto thine own understanding. Matthew had come here angry, running from God. God had met him here and was still directing his paths. Possibly to this place that he'd originally run from. Parker loved the irony in that.

She could see that he might be right. The two of them had needed to meet here, to find forgiveness and a way to move on.

Her phone rang. She glanced at the caller ID and knew she had to take the call.

"I'm going to take this and then head to the nursery to get Faith."

"I'll meet up with you later."

As she walked away she answered. "Parker Smythe."

"Parker, this is Marci. I know you'd planned on being here at the end of June, but we're going to need you in Destin in three weeks. I'm sorry to bother you on the weekend about this, but we have to fill the roster."

"Has something happened?" Parker asked, unsure of how to answer. The idea of leaving now, of leaving Faith…and Matthew… It shouldn't have been this way. She should have come to town, done her job and left according to plan. Now it felt complicated. It felt like heartbreak.

"We've lost one of our nurses. She accepted a permanent placement. Is this going to be a problem?"

"No, of course not." The words hurt, physically hurt.

"That's good to hear, because for a minute, I thought maybe you were going to back out on us."

She bit down on her bottom lip to keep from saying what she felt. She wanted to back out. She wanted to stay. The idea of leaving… She shook her head at the thought of walking away from people she loved. And she did love Matthew. She loved him and needed to be in his life and in Faith's life.

Unfortunately, she couldn't un-hear the words she'd heard twice from the man she loved. Despite his fast proposal the other day, she knew she was his best friend. Always the best friend. She deserved more than that.

"Parker?"

"I'm here. Sorry, I'm at church. No, I'm not backing out on you."

She said her good-byes and stood at the nursery door, watching as one of the workers rocked a toddler. Another held Faith, talking to the baby girl and then laughing at whatever response the infant had given.

"Hey, there's Mama." The worker holding Faith stood and carried the baby to the door. "Look who is here to get you, sweet girl. That's right, Mama is here."

Parker managed a watery smile.

"There's that baby girl!" A woman came to stand next to Faith. Tall, thin and with her hair dyed a silvery lavender.

"Kylie! I didn't know you were coming here," Parker said as she accepted a hug from Matthew's one-time sister-in-law, the ex-wife of Mark Rivers.

"Well, I had to hear my brother-in-law preach. And Junie loves it here. We've actually slipped in at the last minute for the past few weeks. It's been good for us. Today's sermon was tough to hear, but it was a good message."

"Yes, it was." She took Faith from the nursery worker. "Where is Junie?"

"She's with a friend. We homeschool, so I hate to break off her socializing too soon. Can I hold that wee baby?" Kylie asked.

"Of course you can." Parker handed Faith over to the other woman.

"She's beautiful. Are you keeping her?" Kylie asked as they walked away.

"No, they've found her a permanent home. I'll be leaving in a few weeks." It was for the best. If she left, she could put this chapter behind her and move on.

"Oh, I thought maybe she would help keep you here longer."

"Sadly, I committed to this job. And she'll be in a wonderful family."

Kylie gave her a long, sympathetic look. "That's going to be tough for you, for her and for Matthew."

"Yes, it'll be tough."

They walked out the back door, to the churchyard where people gathered to talk and where children ran and played. One of those children was Junie. She was five and dark-haired, like her father, her uncles, her grandfather. It was easy to spot Matthew's niece. Easier because Buck stood nearby, watching her play.

"Interesting how people change," Kylie said. "Buck is growing on me. I guess that is me changing."

"Yes, people change."

"I thought maybe something had changed between you and Matthew." Kylie still held Faith. She smiled down at the infant in her arms. "You are absolutely precious."

"We're still just friends," Parker informed the other woman.

"That's probably for the best. The Rivers men are broken and I'm not sure if they can be fixed. Matthew is a decent man. Mark is like his father. He finds joy in the bottom of the whiskey bottle."

"I'm sorry," Parker sympathized. "As for Matthew, I've always known we were just friends."

"Really? I always thought there was more between the two of you. You were inseparable in high school."

"I'm the best friend. I think that's my lot in life." She said it with a smile.

Kylie gave her a long look and shook her head. "I think you've forgotten who you are."

Now Parker was confused. "I'm sorry?"

Kylie handed her back the baby wrapped in her pale pink blanket, a pink bow on her head. "Parker Smythe, you're a child of the King and that makes you a princess. You're fearfully and wonderfully created. You're fantastically beautiful, inside and out."

"I..." She didn't know what to say.

"Sorry, sometimes I feel the need to say something and it just comes out like that." Kylie gave her a quick hug. "Believe in yourself. That doesn't mean you have to fall in love, get married or even stay in Sunset Ridge. It just means, stop doubting who you were created to be."

She hugged the other woman back. "Thank you."

"Gotta run, my little darling is waving me down. Come have coffee with me."

Kylie started to go, but she stopped, put a hand to her head and seemed to breathe deeply.

"Kylie, are you okay?" Parker hurried to her side.

"I'm good. I didn't eat breakfast. But thank you."

Parker watched the other woman until she met up with her daughter and the two joined hands and hurried across the lawn to the parking lot. She wanted to feel sorry for Kylie Rivers and her daughter, but maybe they were better off without Mark. They had a pretty house, the coffee shop and this community.

They had roots here in Sunset Ridge. Those roots were what Parker had always wanted. She wanted to settle down somewhere and never move again.

As she turned back toward the church, she saw Matthew on the steps talking to Brody Stringer. The younger man had a wide grin on his face, clearly telling a story because whatever he said had Matthew laughing. Matthew glanced her way and waved. For a moment she wondered what it would be like to stay here in Sunset Ridge, to be the person he always turned to, to be the mom who raised Faith.

It all seemed like too much of a dream. She didn't want to hope for all of those things and lose them. It was easier to move on. Taking chances always seemed to end badly for her.

Chapter Fourteen

Two weeks later, Parker packed to take Faith for her second visit with the Jansens. This time the visit would last for four days. From Friday through Tuesday morning. As she changed Faith into a romper, she talked to the baby while fighting tears.

"Oh, baby girl, I do love you. I am praying so hard for you, for your life and the people who will raise you. I've even prayed it could be me, but I don't know if that would be fair to you." She picked the baby up and gave her a kiss. "I'm going to miss you this week."

It wouldn't be easy to let Faith go for the four days, but to keep her mind busy, she'd made reservations to fly to Destin. She needed to check on new accommodations, visit the hospital and definitely take a walk on the beach. Maybe the beach would take away the overwhelming feeling of sadness that clung to her these days.

The days had been longer because she rarely talked to Matthew. He had been busy with Buck and with cattle. She'd been busy with work and Faith. He also helped with Faith, but they met in passing. If she needed him, he would stay at the camper with Faith while Parker worked an evening shift.

Everything had changed between them. She couldn't face him without thinking of his suggestion that they marry in order to keep Faith. No woman wanted that proposal. It was a "solution to a problem" proposal, not an "I can't live without you" proposal.

Faith grinned at her and made sweet cooing sounds that brought Parker back to the present and the baby in her arms. She kissed Faith's cheeks until she giggled just a tiny bit and then she placed the baby in her car seat.

"There we go, pumpkin. Time for you to go see Vicky." Mommy. Vicky would be her mommy. Parker's stomach clenched and she felt the sting of tears. "Nope, we aren't going to cry. Sometimes it hurts to do the right thing."

She wished for Matthew to be making this drive with her. Unfortunately, Buck had a doctor's appointment for his knee surgery and with the weeks it took to get one of those appointments, they couldn't cancel. She wouldn't see them before she left today.

With a quick inspection, she left the camper. She'd already put her bag and Faith's in the car. The only thing left to do was leave. It felt like walking away from a home she'd come to love. Yes, it was just a camper and yes, she would be back in less than a week, but she'd miss it. All too soon, she would leave for good.

She put Faith's seat in the car and snapped it into the base, then she gave Pete a friendly pat and promised to see him soon. She'd come to love the dog, maybe because for most of her life they hadn't had pets. They'd moved too often and they'd never known from town to town if they'd live in a place that accepted pets.

Pete followed her to the driver's side and then he backed away and sat down to watch her leave.

When she arrived at the Jansens' home outside of Tulsa, it was just after ten in the morning. Vicky Jansen, her rounded belly cute in her leggings and tunic top, met Parker at the door. Parker liked the other woman. She thought they probably could have been friends, given time and different circumstances.

"Hey, Parker, come on in. Do you have time for coffee?" Vicky smiled at Faith. Parker had taken her out of the seat and she held her out to the other woman, whose arms were open and ready for the baby.

"I can't. I have to get to the airport. Do you need her seat or just her bag?"

"Just the bag this time. We bought a seat so we wouldn't have to switch back and forth. Where are you off to?"

"Destin, to check on my new job and apartment."

Vicky kissed Faith's cheek. "You smell good, Faith. And I'm jealous. I want to go to the beach. Bring us back a seashell."

"I will. Let me get her bag." Parker hurried away, her heart aching with longing and loss. She grabbed Faith's bag out of the back and the stuffed elephant that she slept with.

"I brought her Warmie," Parker said as she put the stuffed animal in the bag with clothes and other necessities. "It goes in the microwave for about forty-five seconds. She loves it."

"I bet she does." Vicky took the bag from Parker and then gave her a soft look of compassion. "I know this isn't easy for you, but I want you to know that we will love her and hug her often and watch over her. And you can call. Please call."

Parker nodded because she couldn't speak. Her throat tightened around all of the words she wanted to say. Loss felt heavy and suffocating. She thought of Matthew and how much easier this would have been with him at her side, with his arm around her, keeping her strong.

"I have to go." Parker finally managed to squeak the words out. "She loves music. 'Jesus Loves Me.' I sing it to her every night."

"I'll sing for her. I promise," Vicky said. She stood in the door as Parker rushed away.

As she backed out of the driveway, Vicky finally stepped inside, closed the door and then gave a final wave. Parker wanted to talk to someone. She thought about calling Matthew. He'd become the first person she thought of—the way he'd been during high school.

Nothing could convince her that her heart wouldn't be broken by loving him. It wasn't worth giving him her whole heart when what he offered was the best friend portion of his.

She called her mother.

"Hey, sweetie," her mom answered.

"Mom…" And then the tears started.

"Oh, Parker, honey. Did you just take Faith to the Jansens?"

"I did. Ugh, this is terrible and it hurts so much. I know I did it for the right reasons. I stepped in when there was no one else and I gave her the love she needed until a family could be found, but this stinks."

"I know it does. Sometimes doing the right thing hurts. Sometimes it's hard to do what is best."

"Is it?"

"What's that?" her mother asked.

"Is it best? It doesn't feel like the best."

"I think that's something you have to pray about. I don't have answers for you, honey. I do know that I raised you to pray."

"I've prayed and prayed and I honestly keep coming back to the fact that this baby deserves a family with two parents, a home, siblings and stability. I'm not those things. If that's God's answer, then that's where I'm at and I'm doing what He called me to do. It hurts, but I know I'll survive it."

"I know you will, too. Is Matthew with you?"

"No, he had to take Buck to an appointment."

Her mom remained silent for a moment and then: "How are things between the two of you?"

"Mom." Parker let a warning tone ease in. "He's just a friend. As a matter of fact, he's made sure that's clear. He even asked me to marry him, as a friend, in order to keep Faith."

She hadn't mentioned that to her mother. Now there was a long and heavy silence as Eleanora Smythe ruminated on what her daughter had shared. Parker felt a smile sneaking up on her. She could still smile. She wasn't so broken that she couldn't be happy.

"Did he?" her mother finally asked. "Well, that's interesting. And you said no?"

"Of course I said no. Mom, he's a friend. That's all. I don't want to marry him just to be married. That wouldn't be the right thing for us or for Faith."

"Why wouldn't he marry you for more than friendship?" her mother asked, obviously clueless about this situation. "It seems to me that the two of you have always had a special relationship, far more than just friends."

"We're just friends. Mom, I really don't want to discuss this."

"I know you don't. Parker, I'm your mother and I'm going to tell you this. Every time you doubt yourself, your worth and your beauty, you're doubting your Creator and the beautiful person He created you to be. You might not see your worth, but He does. You're running away again and I wish you would stay and see this through."

"I'm not running away. I've never run from anything."

Her mother sighed, long and pointed. "You use this job as an excuse to keep moving and to keep from forming relationships with people because relationships are tough and sometimes hurt. Honey, it's a part of life. We find joy and love and heartache, all in the same big package."

"I know," she whispered. "Oh, Mom, I do love you and I'm thankful for your wisdom. I just can't stay in Sunset Ridge. It hurts too much. Also, eventually Matthew will leave. He's working through the pain and I think he will return to his church in Chicago."

"So you do love him?"

She paused, and then answered with the truth. "I do." She didn't cry. Instead she felt at peace. She loved Matthew. She could live with that. "I have to go. I'm catching a flight in two hours."

"When you come back, stop and see us. I'll make no-bake cookies."

Parker almost said no, but why should she deny herself something she loved—her parents and the cookies. "I'll take you up on that."

Thirty minutes later she had parked her car and was heading through the airport. Her phone rang. She glanced down, didn't recognize the number and kept walking. She didn't have time to talk to a telemarketer or a politician who wanted her vote.

If it had been Matthew, she might have answered. Or maybe she wouldn't have. In the coming weeks their relationship would change. Faith would be with her new family, Parker would be in Destin and Matthew would figure out his life. They wouldn't be in day-to-day contact. They wouldn't have a baby girl to hold them together. The reunion, brought about by a tiny baby girl left in a truck, would be over.

Matthew walked through the back door of the house, kicked off his boots and left them next to the washer. He washed his hands in the utility sink and stripped off the shirt that he'd ruined pulling a calf. He hoped this day wasn't one of many, because it had been rough.

When he'd gotten home from taking Buck to the doctor, he'd discovered the empty camper with a note from Parker telling him she'd be back next week. Then he'd discovered the cow struggling to give birth. He'd spent a good hour helping deliver her calf with Buck standing by shouting orders.

Just like old times.

"What do you want for supper?" Buck yelled from the kitchen.

"I don't really care," Matthew answered as he grabbed a towel to dry his arms and then pulled on a clean shirt.

He entered the kitchen where Buck was sitting on

the seat of the rolling walker, rummaging through the fridge. Buck glanced up, surveying him with unmistakable compassion. Matthew didn't know how to handle this version of Buck.

From the front of the house, the door slammed, and Pete barked.

"You expecting company?" Matthew asked his dad, wary because they never had unexpected guests.

"Nope," Buck answered, pushing to his feet and grabbing the handles of the walker.

"Dad, you in there?" a female voice called out.

"Well, I'll be. It's Jael. I'm in the kitchen," Buck shouted.

She entered, the princess of the Rivers and Bowen families. Jael was tall, slim and dark-haired. Her silver eyes matched the silvery streaks in her hair. She had a tattoo on one arm: a rose swirling with thorns. She was a wild child who somehow managed to function as a juvenile officer in the Tulsa area.

"Well, look who is here. My dearest older brother. Give me a hug." She hurried to him and wrapped thin but strong arms around him. "Since you wouldn't come see me, I came to see you."

"How long you here for?" Buck asked.

"Not long, but once you have your surgery, I'm taking a leave of absence and moving in to help take care of you. I figured Matthew would be ready to get back to Chicago and his church."

"I'm not sure if he's going back. I've been waiting for him to leave for the past month or so but he doesn't seem to be in a hurry."

Matthew rolled his eyes at that. "I've been helping."

Buck waved a hand around. "Of course you have. I just didn't think you'd stay this long."

"I guess if Jael is here, I can leave anytime."

"I didn't say you had to go," Buck grumbled. "I kind of like having you here. I'm pretty proud I didn't have to pull that calf."

"I bet you are."

Jael poured herself a glass of iced sweet tea. "What's for supper?"

"We were just discussing that." Buck rubbed his chin. "I think maybe we'll have sausage and fried taters."

"My favorite," Jael said a little too gleefully.

For Matthew, this all played out a little strangely. Buck cooking supper. Jael, dark and somber to look at, but strangely cheerful and bubbly. He didn't know her well enough to really make a judgment on her personality.

His phone rang. He answered and walked away from the two busybodies who obviously wanted to listen in.

"Matthew, it's Jerry. I know this is short notice and you have a lot on your plate," the church deacon started and then he paused. "Well, we were just wondering if you might preach for the next month. Honestly, Matthew, if we thought you'd stay in Sunset Ridge, we'd make an offer to keep you as a full-time pastor."

Jerry rambled on for a bit and then he took a breath. The whole time he talked, Matthew tried to keep moving to avoid his sister.

"Well, what do you think?" Jerry asked after a long speech that Matthew heard little of.

"I'm not sure," he answered honestly. "I'm supposed to fly up to Chicago at the end of the month to talk to our church board and my pastoral staff."

"I know we're small potatoes, but if you felt you could even give us a couple of weeks? The deacons also wondered if you might be able to help us find a pastor. You might have connections within the ministry, someone willing to come to a small town and help us keep this little church vital and relevant for this world we live in."

"Let me think on it," Matthew offered. "I do have some connections. Even within our church, we might have someone called to minister in a small church."

"Matthew, I appreciate that. We all appreciate you for helping us out."

Matthew ended the call and he realized that something profound had happened in the past week or so—acceptance. He'd finally come to a place of acceptance. He would always miss his friend. He might always wonder why, but something deep inside had shifted and he knew that God was working all things together for good. The hospital chaplain job, the preaching at the local church—these were temporary gigs, as if God were allowing him to slowly test his faith and see that it still shone true, even if its light had dimmed for a while.

Expectancy simmered because he knew, beyond a shadow of a doubt, that God had been at work behind the scenes, bringing together His plan and His will.

"What's that smile for?" Jael asked, her eyes shrewd.

"I bet you're good at your job," he said as he sidestepped her and headed back to the kitchen.

Buck looked up from where he sat slicing potatoes. "What was that all about?"

"The church wants me to help them find a pastor."

"They've given up on getting you to accept the position, I guess?" Buck said as he aggressively cut the potatoes.

"Not completely, but I think they realize I can't."

"Don't know why not," Buck said.

"Because I have a church, a home, a life in Chicago."

"Do you really? Because it can't be much of a life if you can walk away for months."

"Don't argue with him," Jael warned Matthew. "He always wins."

"Yeah, I know he does."

Buck ignored them and reached to turn the last dial knob radio on the planet to a country music station. Maybe not the last, but it had definitely been in this kitchen for a good thirty years or longer.

"You could marry that little gal and stay here and preach." Buck hadn't finished arguing.

"Her name is Parker."

"Parker Smythe?" Jael asked.

Matthew ignored them. His phone rang again and he used it as an excuse to leave the room and their badgering and their ideas about what he should do with his life. He glanced at the phone, a little hopeful that their mention of Parker had meant something. It wasn't Parker, so he didn't answer. They could leave a message.

He guessed he'd better get used to not having Parker around every day. Or at all.

Selfishly, he prayed that she'd open her eyes and realize he loved her. Maybe he should have told her?

Maybe he should stop doubting what God could do—what he'd already done—in his life and his family. It only took a few days around Buck to realize that God truly could do anything. If he believed that, why couldn't he believe that God would help him to be the man Parker deserved?

She deserved more than a "best friend" proposal. She deserved to be loved and cherished by a man who would stay by her side forever. And who was willing to actually say those things to her.

Chapter Fifteen

Parker didn't last five days in Destin. She was walking the beach on the third day when she realized how much she missed Faith. She missed Matthew. She didn't know what that meant or what would happen, but she made a few calls, changed her flight and left Florida the next day.

As she hurried to her car in the parking lot of the Tulsa Airport, she considered calling Vicky on the off chance they were at home and they might let her see Faith. If not, maybe she'd go home to her parents for a night and try again tomorrow.

Vicky and Daron were going to raise Faith. She had accepted that. She knew that they were good for the baby girl and would raise her in church and with every opportunity. Parker would accept visits if they didn't mind. Perhaps she could be in the baby's life as an honorary aunt. She could bring birthday and Christmas gifts, maybe take her for pedicures when she got a little older.

She would also have to decide what to do about Matthew. If he went back to Chicago, would they visit or at least talk on the phone? Maybe sometimes get together for lunch when she was in his area? Or would he come back to visit Sunset Ridge?

The phone rang five times. She counted. On the sixth, she nearly hung up. On the seventh it was answered by a groggy sounding Vicky. Parker glanced at her watch. It was four in the afternoon. Surely, she hadn't gotten the other woman up?

"Vicky, it's Parker. I hope I didn't bother you, but I'm back early and I wanted to see if I could visit Faith."

She waited, holding her breath, anticipation crawling through her.

"Oh, Parker, I didn't expect to hear from you. I'm so sorry." Vicky sighed and it sounded as if she might be in pain.

"Sorry?" Parker didn't understand. "Do you mean I can't see her?"

"Oh, no, that's not it at all," Vicky said. "Parker, I've been having contractions and I'm on bed rest. I don't have Faith."

Parker's skin felt chilled and a nervous shiver raced down her spine. "Where is she?"

"I'm sorry. I don't know. Jackie explained that once we turned her back to the state, we were no longer involved in her case and couldn't have that information. I didn't want to have to do that, but I couldn't keep her. It was the worst thing, giving her up."

"When did this happen?" Parker grabbed her bag and hurried through the airport, needing to find her car and find Faith as soon as possible.

"This morning. I'm so sorry. It wasn't fair to her to come into a home where she would have to be taken care of by others. I didn't want to let her go and I hope you'll understand and forgive me."

"Vicky, oh, no, please don't. You tried and for right now, you have to worry about that little baby inside you. You need to focus your energy on staying healthy. No one blames you for that. I'll find Faith."

Vicky hesitated for a few seconds. "I know you will. Parker, she wasn't meant to be ours and I think you know that."

Parker stopped abruptly and let the other woman's words sink in. "I know." It hit her hard. She'd messed things up. "I thought I was doing the right thing."

"There's always another opportunity to do the right thing," Vicky encouraged.

"Vicky, I have to go, but if you need anything, please let me know. I'll be praying for you all."

After ending the call, she raced to her car, her breath heaving as she reached it. She really needed to start exercising again!

Spots danced before her eyes. She leaned against her car, catching her breath, and then she unlocked it and tossed her bag in the back seat. The seat that still held Faith's car seat.

As she drove toward Sunset Ridge, not even sure why she was going in that direction, she tried to call Jackie. No answer. The only solution seemed to be to get to Matthew and perhaps they could track the baby down.

Their baby. She didn't care what they had to do to keep her. Maybe she would have to proclaim her love to Matthew a second time, risk the embarrassment and take a chance. She smiled at her reflection in the mirror.

"You, Kid, are fearfully and wonderfully created. Don't forget that. You're beautiful."

She giggled, because she hadn't done or said anything so ridiculous in a long time.

As she pulled up the drive to the Rocking R, she started to relax. Peace swept over her. It felt like coming home. Maybe she'd buy a little house in Sunset Ridge, work at the local doctor's office or the hospital in Wagoner. Maybe she'd raise Faith on her own?

Matthew might stay in the area and be a father figure to the little girl and a helper when Parker needed him. That made more sense than rushing into his house and proclaiming her love. That simply couldn't happen twice in her lifetime. The humiliation of rejection wasn't her cup of tea.

Matthew. What if he wasn't here? What if he'd gone to Chicago?

Nope, she wasn't going there. *Peace. Be still.* She took a deep breath and allowed the peace to overflow her spirit.

There was a strange car in the driveway. Two cars, actually. She parked and got out, then gave Pete a pat on the head as she walked up the steps of the porch. There were lights on in the living room and she could hear voices raised in conversation. She'd never seen the house so bright or lived in.

She knocked on the door and waited.

A moment later the door swung open. A woman with dark, silver-streaked hair stood before her. She seemed familiar but Parker couldn't place her.

"Parker! Wow, now this is a surprise."

Parker blinked. "I'm sorry? Do I know you?"

The woman pulled her into a quick hug. "Nope, but I know you. Social media—isn't that how we all creep on people we want to know more about?"

"Creepy is the right word for it," Parker mused, trying to see past the other woman. "Is Matthew here?"

"Yes, he is. By the way, I'm his sister, Jael."

"Oh, Jael, it's nice to meet you." Nice, but at the moment, disconcerting and a bit overwhelming.

"Come on in." Jael motioned her in. Parker was aware of the sweep of her hand, of jewelry and a deep red manicure. "Pete, stay out."

Pete sat, but he whined about not being given entrance to his domain.

"The dog drives me crazy," Jael admitted as she led Parker through the house. "He sheds a small dog every day. It's disgusting. Matthew is in the family room."

The house had a family room?

Jael grinned as she pushed the door open and motioned Parker in ahead of her. Parker didn't know what to make of the younger woman. They had met briefly when Jael had been a child during the rare times she'd visited the ranch to spend a weekend with her father and brothers. She'd been an energetic girl who demanded a lot and seldom seemed to appreciate what her brothers, specifically Matthew, did for her.

It seemed that she'd changed. People often did.

"Go on in," Jael ordered.

"I'm not sure," Parker said.

Fear. She'd met the rascal a few times in her life. It took hold, telling her she couldn't walk through that door. She couldn't face Matthew. She couldn't handle the idea of losing Faith. Sure, she'd driven here specifically for his help, but now that the reality of her impulsive visit was upon her, she wondered if she'd done the right thing.

"You should go in there," Jael chided. "Come on.

Big girl pants. Wear a smile and confidence and get in there."

Parker gave the other woman a look, and then she laughed because Jael Rivers was a hot mess, but so far she liked her.

"Right. Confidence and big girl pants."

Parker walked through the door. The first person she spotted happened to be the missing caseworker, Jackie. She scanned the room until her gaze fixed on Matthew. He looked a little surprised to see her. As he studied her, he also handed papers to Jackie. That's when Parker saw the bassinet, the one she'd left in the camper.

Parker had never been the fainting type, but the moment called for a little wooziness. She reached for the back of a nearby chair and took a breath until the stars faded from her vision.

"She might keel over," Jael said from what seemed like a million miles away. The hand with the long, red nails circled Parker's upper arm, offering support.

Matthew started toward her, his smile so genuine, so heart-stopping. She wanted to say something, but she didn't know what to say. Her gaze went from Matthew to the bassinet. Jackie stood, reached in and pulled out the infant girl that had stolen Parker's heart.

"Welcome back," Matthew said softly as he approached. "I didn't expect you."

"No," she said. "You have Faith. Vicky said she didn't know who had her."

"Jackie called me this morning. It took me about two minutes to make a decision."

"What decision did you make?" Her heart felt as if it might be holding still, waiting for his answer.

"I made a decision to stay here, to pastor a little country church and raise Faith."

Parker remained still, needing to hear more about his dreams for the future, because hers were so similar. She didn't know what he meant to say, but she knew that the next few minutes mattered for eternity.

"They just handed her over to you?" Parker said it softly but with a bit of her old self in the words.

Matthew couldn't help but grin at Parker's question. "I'm a responsible adult. Most of the time."

"Yes, I know you are, but they don't typically just hand over foster children," she responded, her cheeks dimpling, her toffee eyes glistening.

"I have been helping to care for her."

"Yes, you have." Parker walked away from him, going to the bassinet. "Can I hold her?"

Jackie picked up her purse. "I'm going to make myself scarce. I'll talk to you tomorrow and we'll see where we go from here."

Parker nodded, watching the caseworker leave before reaching into the bassinet for the baby. As she held her, Matthew shooed his nosy little sister from the room.

Parker kissed Faith's cheeks and the baby gave her a sloppy smile. "You are the sweetest thing." Then she gave Matthew another look as she cuddled the baby close. "You're going to stay here and raise her."

She sounded a little put out by that. He needed to reassure her. He needed to go forward with his idea, praying he hadn't completely misunderstood what he thought God wanted him to do.

"That's my plan. I told Jackie that I'm sure the two

of us can do this and give Faith all of the love any child should have."

"You want to share her?" Parker bit down on her bottom lip as she studied the baby in her arms. "I thought about that after talking to Vicky. I thought maybe we could go back to doing this the way we'd been doing it. I'm going to buy a place here. I'm tired of moving."

Relief flooded him as she said those words. He'd worried that she would be so determined to stick to her plan, she wouldn't consider his.

He studied her for a moment. She held Faith gently, her eyes glowing with love for the baby. And Faith loved her. They had a bond and the baby hadn't forgotten her.

He wanted to always be the one to make Parker look this happy. He wanted to see that look of love in her eyes, for Faith and for him. Selfish of him, but he couldn't help what he wanted.

"I do want us to raise her. Together. I don't want you to buy a place of your own."

"You might eventually want your camper back," she said.

He liked when she was clueless. It gave her a beautiful naive expression that he wanted to kiss away.

"I don't want my camper back," he informed her.

She looked up at him, sweetly unsure. Her lips parted as if she meant to say something. He couldn't miss this moment.

He leaned to kiss her cheek, then her lips, holding her loosely so as not to crush Faith between them. She kissed him back, one arm going to his neck. Her touch grounded him, made him aware of just how perfect she was for him.

Eventually the kiss ended and she rested her head

on his shoulder. "I came here intending to be brave, to be fierce and to tell you that I love you. I can be your best friend, Matthew, but I'm the friend who loves you. I can't raise this baby with you except in the way we've already been doing it because I want more from a relationship than sharing Faith."

She obviously needed more because she wasn't understanding what he wanted. He wanted her. He loved her.

"Parker Smythe, I want us. I want the three of us, together. I'm asking you again to be my wife and to make Faith our daughter."

"We can't get married just to adopt her." She stared at him with hurt and sadness in her eyes.

"Are you…" He shook his head and stopped. He was messing this up again. Gently, he took Faith from her arms and placed her in the bassinet with her elephant Warmie.

"Parker, let me start over. This isn't about Faith. This is about us. This is about *our* life together. I've lived life without you and life with you. The days without you are long and miserable. I want you at my side for the rest of my life. I want us to raise Faith as our daughter, because she deserves two parents who love each other and love her. Please say that you'll marry me. Not for Faith, but because we're meant to be a family. I love you."

It felt so good to finally say those words to her that he laughed and repeated them. "I love you, Parker Smythe, and I want to spend my life with you, in this little town, in our little country church."

Her warm brown eyes were glossy with unshed tears. If she said no…

He couldn't even think about it. That wasn't an option.

* * *

Parker didn't know what to say. She didn't know how to react. Matthew stood before her, his eyes—his expression—reflecting his words. He held a black box in his hand and as she tried to catch up with everything happening, he opened the box.

Inside the box, a necklace glimmered, stray beams of sunlight dancing off the diamonds nestled in golden leaves. She gasped. Her heart stuttered, making it difficult to fight the tears that welled up.

It looked like her grandmother's necklace. A necklace she kept in a safe at her mother's house.

He removed it from the box and fastened it around her neck. "I asked your dad's blessing on this proposal. Believe it or not, I'm old-fashioned that way. Your mother gave me a necklace that had belonged to your grandmother. She said that once upon a time it had a matching ring that was meant to be yours, but the ring got lost. It took some searching, but I found a matching ring."

She touched the ring he held out, longing to find words to convey what this gesture meant to her. Surely a person who cared for babies, cranky cats and elderly teachers could be careful with her heart. She looked up to find his eyes on hers.

"It's beautiful," she told him, aching to wear the ring.

She was going to blubber and then she'd be blotchy and have a red nose.

"I want you to wear it," he told her. "I want you to have this ring that has been crafted to stand the test of time, to symbolize that we can also stand the test of time. Like these diamonds, we can undergo the pressures of life, but be made more beautiful."

"You're going to make me cry," she said. "I'm an ugly crier."

She took a step closer, needing his nearness, needing his words. He was beautiful in ways that didn't make sense, not only because God had gifted him with a rather amazing face, but because he was, deep down, good.

She loved him. She always had and always would.

"We have been through the fire," she told him.

"And we're strong enough to withstand whatever comes our way. As long as we're together and as long as we trust God with our future, we're going to be okay, Parker."

He lifted a hand to stroke her cheek. His mesmerizing eyes caught and held hers. She couldn't move, could barely breathe.

"Parker, you're the love of my life *and* my best friend. Would you consider marrying a farmer, a small-town preacher, a man who adores you and wants to raise a sweet little girl with you?"

She wanted to be brave enough to say yes, to believe him. She wanted the dream with him, with Faith. When she thought of forever with a man, it had only ever been Matthew Rivers that she dreamed of.

He bent to whisper close to her ear. "This is the part where you're supposed to say yes." She could hear laughter in his voice.

A lifetime with this funny, intelligent, gentle man.

"Yes. I will marry you." She leaned into his embrace. "I love you, Matthew. I never stopped, even when I wanted to."

"I love you, too. And I regret that there was a time when I couldn't accept those words, didn't feel I deserved them or could live up to them. I'm ready to be the man you deserve."

Faith's faint cry ended the moment. Parker peeked over Matthew's shoulder at the little girl who would be theirs. Before she could go to the baby, he took her hand and slid the ring on her finger, then kissed it for good measure.

Parker knew that from this day forward, life would never be the same. It wouldn't always be easy. It would never be perfect. It would be filled with laughter and tears.

But more laughter. Maybe loving them was a risk, but these two? They would always be worth it. Because this love was for keeps.

Epilogue

Almost Six Months Later

It was a Christmas wedding, or nearly Christmas. The church had been decorated for the holidays with twinkling lights, white and red poinsettias and holly.

Parker waited in the vestibule with Buck and the wedding party at her side. Her future father-in-law was feeling pretty energetic since his knee replacement. He'd taken to riding horses again. He loved to play chase with Junie and he often carried Faith around his house, talking to her and singing to her. He'd even found recipes for organic baby food that he made in his gourmet kitchen and he had hopes of marketing in Kylie's Bakery.

Who knew Buck would be an entrepreneur?

Parker had been living on the new property, the old Jackson place. The craftsman house had been remodeled and she'd spent the past month decorating, buying furniture and preparing for move in day. It would be their home together, hers, Matthew's and Faith's. And maybe someday there would be more children.

She hoped to fill the four bedroom house with family, love and laughter.

Today was the beginning of their lives together.

"Are you almost ready?" he asked.

"I am," she whispered, shaking out the train of her white velvet dress.

Junie danced around in her pale rose outfit, letting the skirt of her dress twirl. She would pull the ring bearer, Faith, down the aisle in a wagon. Kylie, Parker's matron of honor, leaned to whisper something in Junie's ear, and the little girl stopped twirling and managed to appear very serious. As the only brother to make it home, Luke was Matthew's best man and he smiled down at his niece while waiting for his cue. Jael loved to sing, and she had a performance for the end of the ceremony that she was warming up for nearby.

Parker peeked through the doors and saw her father place his Bible on the pulpit and then walk toward her. He and Buck would both escort her to the altar, and her father would perform the ceremony.

"I'm sure proud you're letting me help walk you down the aisle," Buck whispered and then he leaned to kiss her cheek. "And I'm right glad to have you for a daughter. If that son of mine ever messes up, you let me know and I'll straighten him out."

"Thank you." She leaned a head on his shoulder, a quick gesture, as the music began to play. Kylie went first, escorted by the handsome and somewhat standoffish Luke Rivers. Next, Junie and Faith. Junie pulled the wagon, stopped to sprinkle flowers, pulled a little farther, more flowers. Halfway down the aisle, she got tired and left the wagon and Faith in the center of the church.

She looked very pleased with herself as she sprinkled flowers and ignored the crying baby.

Parker put a hand to her face as a ripple of laughter went through the guests. "What do we do?"

Buck pointed. Near the front of the church sat Jackie, their caseworker, and she hurried to the wagon and the crying baby. She said something silly, played peekaboo and then pulled the wagon the rest of the way down the aisle.

The wedding march played. Buck and her father walked her through the doors. Buck did a little jig and then he straightened up and sedately did his part. At the end of the aisle, her father kissed her cheek and stepped forward to perform the ceremony. Her heart overflowed with blessings, joy, faith and love.

Buck stepped away and Matthew took his place. His smile cherished her as he looked down at her and then he gave her a slow, lazy wink that made her giggle. "I love you," she whispered.

He whispered the same and bent to drop a kiss on her cheek.

Martin Smythe cleared his throat. "At this point in the ceremony, I usually ask who gives this bride." He cleared his throat again and chuckled. "Today I respond that her mother and I give her."

"Thank you," Matthew told her father and then her mother. "For this gift of a remarkable wife to love, honor and cherish, I thank you."

"Stop," Parker whispered to the man who, after today, would be her husband. "Let's get this over with so we can begin to live our lives together."

Matthew put a finger to his lips. "Shhh."

They both laughed and a ripple of amusement spread through the crowd.

Her father took the rings from the pillow in Faith's lap. He held them up and explained that a ring is gold and a circle. The gold being incorruptible. The circle, having no end.

They repeated their vows and added a few words of their own about the strength of their love and the friendship that would get them through the difficult times.

After they'd repeated "I do," her father gave Matthew permission to kiss the bride.

Matthew pulled Parker close and touched his lips to hers, melting her with the sweetness of his love for her. She loved him back. Matthew was her best friend. When no one else noticed her, he had. He'd looked beneath the surface to the person who loved him.

"Hey, did I miss the wedding?" The voice came from the back of the church. It wasn't a particularly sober voice. "Well, I'm in time for the congratulations."

Everyone turned to stare. Matthew pulled back, giving his brother a look. "Mark, you're making an entrance."

"That's what I do best, bro." Mark glanced around at the crowd. "Uh-oh, I guess I ruined this here black-tie affair. Well, I am your friend in the lowest places." Mark caught sight of his wife and his stricken daughter. "Hey, girls, I'm home."

Luke headed back down the aisle to corral his brother. Something was said about Mark needing help. After that it was a scuffle and then Luke "helped" Mark out of the building.

Matthew pulled his wife close and kissed her again.

"Welcome to the family," he said, and she smiled and squeezed his arm. "I love you, Parker Rivers."

"Great, I sound like a state park." She giggled and pulled him closer.

"I love parks," he whispered, and he kissed her again.

"I love cake," Junie said. She looked a little teary.

Matthew picked her up and tossed her in the air. "Then let's have a reception."

Jackie brought Faith to join them and Parker took the little girl in her arms and held her close.

"I have a gift for you," Jackie said in a solemn voice. "The week before Christmas, we go to court to make the three of you a forever family. Congratulations."

Matthew pulled her close and she sniffed away the tears. This was a happy day, a day of rejoicing and not of tears.

Together they made their way from the sanctuary to face the future. A family.

* * * * *

Dear Reader,

Parker and Matthew share a special relationship—a love based on friendship. I believe the best relationships are built on the foundation of friendship. When times are difficult, when we hit rocky patches, knowing that your partner is also your best friend is a blessing.

I hope you enjoyed *Reunited by the Baby* and its message of hope, of acceptance and of true love. I enjoyed creating these characters, watching them grow in faith, accepting loss and learning to love others and themselves.

Brenda Minton

COMING NEXT MONTH FROM
Love Inspired

THEIR AMISH SECRET
Amish Country Matches • by Patricia Johns

Putting the past behind her is all single Amish mother Claire Glick wants. But when old love Joel Beiler shows up on her doorstep in the middle of a harrowing storm, it could jeopardize everything she's worked for—including her best-kept secret...

THE QUILTER'S SCANDALOUS PAST
by Patrice Lewis

Esther Yoder's family must sell their mercantile store, and when an out-of-town buyer expresses interest, Esther is thrilled. Then she learns the buyer is Joseph Kemp—the man responsible for ruining her reputation. Can she set aside her feelings for the sake of the deal?

THE RANCHER'S SANCTUARY
K-9 Companions • by Linda Goodnight

With zero ranching experience, greenhorn Nathan Garrison has six months to reopen an abandoned guest ranch—or lose it forever. So he hires scarred cowgirl Monroe Matheson to show him the ropes. As they work together, will secrets from the past ruin their chance at love?

THE BABY INHERITANCE
Lazy M Ranch • by Tina Radcliffe

Life changes forever when rancher Drew Morgan inherits his best friend's baby. But when he learns professor Sadie Ross is also part of the deal, things get complicated. Neither one of them is ready for domestic bliss, but sweet baby Mae might change their minds...

MOTHER FOR A MONTH
by Zoey Marie Jackson

Career-weary Sienna King yearns to become a mother, and opportunity knocks when know-it-all reporter Joel Armstrong comes to her with an unusual proposal. Putting aside their differences, they must work together to care for his infant nephew, but what happens when their pretend family starts to feel real?

THE NANNY NEXT DOOR
Second Chance Blessings • by Jenna Mindel

Grieving widower Jackson Taylor moves to small-town Michigan for the sake of his girls. When he hires his attractive next-door neighbor, Maddie Williams, to be their nanny, it could be more than he bargained for as the line between personal and professional starts to blur...

LOOK FOR THESE AND OTHER LOVE INSPIRED BOOKS WHEREVER BOOKS ARE SOLD, INCLUDING MOST BOOKSTORES, SUPERMARKETS, DISCOUNT STORES AND DRUGSTORES.

LICNM0323